"And that is another thing you will have to learn," he said softly. "To allow a gentleman to assist you, even if you can do it yourself."

"Always? Must I always allow every gentleman that comes along to assist me . . . ?" She was being coy. She knew that she was, but couldn't help herself.

"No," he said firmly and had his arms around her as his mouth closed on hers. Her lips were sweet and her body tempted him to crush her in his hold. His kiss lingered into another, teaching her to respond. When he let her up for air, she managed a smile and said softly, "Is that another thing I must learn?"

"No again, love. You need no lesson there. . . ."

Fawcett Books
by Claudette Williams:

DESERT ROSE . . . ENGLISH MOON

LACEY

LADY BELL

LADY MADCAP

LORD WILDFIRE

REGENCY STAR

SASSY

SONG OF SILKIE

SWEET DISORDER

# LADY
# MADCAP

## Claudette Williams

FAWCETT CREST • NEW YORK

A Fawcett Crest Book
Published by Ballantine Books
Copyright © 1987 by Claudette Williams

Library of Congress Catalog Card Number: 87-90841

ISBN 0-449-20981-4

Manufactured in the United States of America

First Edition: September 1987

Dedicated to Gordon with love, for all the good times . . .

Claudy

# Chapter One

Scott Hanover did not stand on ceremony when visiting Easton Manor. In fact, no one at the manor could remember a time when he had. Perhaps this was due to his boyish charm, or the warmth of his smile, or the undeniable truth that he was held in open affection by Miss Easton and all her staff. There, too, the Easton staff had watched their young mistress and Scott play in nearly every room of the elegant country manor from the moment they were able to crawl until the present. Therefore, it was with easy style that Scott Hanover marched past Dasset into the open hall and called in stentorian accents, "Flip, you madcap . . . where are you?" He waited a long moment and then turned to Dasset, the manor's tall and portly butler, to inquire, "Where has she gone off to now? She was supposed to meet me by the pike twenty minutes ago."

Dasset sighed and shook his head. "Something dreadful has happened, sir. It was the morning mail."

Scott's dark blond brows drew together over his grey-blue eyes. "Dreadful . . . ? What do you mean? Where is she?"

1

"Miss Felicia was overset by something she received in the morning mail." Dasset attempted to explain. It was not his place to confide his mistress's business to anyone, but Scott was not just anyone. Why, he often thought of the boy as he might have thought of Miss Felicia's brother, if she had been fortunate enough to have one, which she had not.

The last two years had been hard on Miss Felicia. She had lost her father more than twenty-three months ago to a sudden stroke, and then some eleven months ago her stepmother had died as well. Felicia had adored her stepmother as well as her natural parent, and the losses had been difficult for her. Scott had stood beside her throughout, and though he was no older than she and both were one and twenty, he shouldered her pain more often than not.

"What?" he asked now. "What is towards?"

"We don't know." Dasset shrugged. "She became extremely agitated and ran out of the house."

"Who was the letter from?"

"From the Duke of Somerset," replied Dasset gravely.

"Good Lord!" ejaculated Scott, putting a hand through his uncovered yellow locks. "What could *he* want?"

"He is her guardian . . . appointed by her stepmother . . . in her stepmother's will," offered Dasset lest Scott had forgotten.

"I know that! But what should he want now? He has never bothered with Flip. All she ever got from him was some curt message after Lady Belinda's funeral." He was frowning darkly. "Which direction did Flip take?"

2

"I am sorry, sir, I didn't see . . . but I don't think she took her horse."

"Right, then . . . I know where she went!" said Scott moving toward the door.

Felicia Easton was nearly twenty-one years old, but sitting with her knees pulled up to her chin in the middle of the wild, grassy field, she looked a veritable child. Her long black hair was loosely blowing in the cool breeze. Her gown was a simple muslin of soft shades of brown. On her feet she wore half boots that were aged but comfortable rather than stylish and pretty.

Her hands hugged her calves in to herself and she sighed out loud. This last piece of news was almost more than she could bear. *He* was coming! He was coming to Easton and he meant to send her to some outlandish place. This was not acceptable. Who did he think he was? How dare he? She was mistress of herself, mistress of her home. Here was this old fidget of a duke who hadn't bothered with her since her stepmother's death, and he suddenly takes it upon himself to command orders on her head? The devil he did!

Why? Why now? For more than ten months he had left her alone, and now with hunting season just around the corner he decides to whisk her off. This was her home. Her parents were gone, but at least she had her home, her beloved setting, familiar and dear . . . and Scott. She wouldn't be taken away!

"There you are, you miserable thing," Scott called out as he jumped the paddock fence and jogged toward her. "Did you forget we were to go into town

3

today and have a look at old man Crull's new black-and-tan?''

Flip heard his voice, scurried with more speed than grace to her feet, and dove at him. ''Scott . . . oh Scott . . . !'' she wailed and buried her pert face into his hard chest.

He frowned and pried her hands from his lapels. ''Eh . . . what's this monkey?''

She sniffed and looked up with soulful eyes. ''He is coming to get me.''

''He is what?'' requested Master Scott. ''Who is coming to get you?''

''The duke!''

''Never say so!'' Scott was moved to ejaculate.

''Well he is,'' wailed Flip, ''and I won't go with him.''

''Where does he mean to take you?'' Scott was frowning in some puzzlement.

''To . . . to . . . Swindon.'' Flip gulped on the thought.

''To Swindon?'' ejaculated Scott in some horror. ''Of all the outlandish places! Why the devil should he take you to Swindon?''

''Says it is not to be thought of . . . my . . . my living here without protection. Says I was a wicked girl for misleading him . . . says . . .''

''Hold!'' Scott put up his hand. ''How the bloody hell did he find out you were unchaperoned?'' His mind searched, and fervently he hoped it had not been his father who had tipped Felicia such a turn.

She looked dolefully up at him and pulled a grimace. ''Old Pudding Face wrote and told him!''

''The dowager Hatfield?'' he growled. ''Why, the old busybody! Didn't think she knew . . . didn't think

4

anyone but m'father knew. Thought we had everyone pretty well diddled.''

"Hmmm." She allowed, "So did I . . . but she has been stopping by more times than I can count and always asking after me . . . wondering about my aunt and why she never sees her about." She sighed. "She must have put it all together, for she wrote to the duke and actually told him I invented a nonexistent aunt." She wrung her hands together. "Scott . . . what am I to do?"

He put his arm about her. "Buck up ol' girl. We'll think of something. Bound to, you know."

"You don't understand. . . . Scott, there isn't any time at all. Somehow this letter must have been delayed in the mail . . . it was written two months ago!"

"Two months ago? Well, then, no doubt the old fidget has forgotten his intentions to fetch you to Swindon."

She eyed him with sudden hope dawning. "Do you think so? Oh, Scott. . . ." Then she frowned and shook her head. "That doesn't make sense, though."

"Doesn't it? Well, writing a letter and saying he would come and take you off and then not showing up doesn't make sense either," he returned pugnaciously.

"Yes, well . . . I have a notion he was delayed by business but will be here at any moment. And when he comes . . . Oh, Scott, I won't go, I tell you I just won't go!"

He looked at her for a long time. This was not something he wanted to do. He adored Felicia. She was his lifelong friend. He was more comfortable with her than with any other person of his acquaintance. There were times, in fact, when he even wanted to try and see what it would be like to kiss her, but there wasn't any passion in his breast when he thought of her, just affection. He was making a sacrifice when his next words hit the wind: "Flip . . . if you marry me . . . you'll never have to leave here . . . or me . . . and I should like that."

She grew watery-eyed again and threw her arms about him. Her words were muffled against his chest. "You big silly love."

He gulped. "Does this mean . . . you accept?"

She laughed and pulled away. "Terrified, eh? No, sap-head, no, I shall spare you and decline your very obliging offer."

"It answers," he returned quietly, though he was much relieved.

"No, it does not. We are friends . . . not lovers."

"We could be both," he responded gallantly.

"Why, Scott . . . that was nicely said. Some girl will be very lucky to have you as husband one day . . . but not I."

He took exception to this. "Why not you?"

"Because, I have already told you, we are friends . . . brother and sister, understand?" She eyed him for her answer and received it in his sheepish smile.

"Aye. I understand . . . but then, what's to do, Flip?"

She linked her arm through his and started walking toward the woodland path that would take them to the stables. "I don't know, Scotty-boy, I just don't know, but I do know this: I won't be taken against my will to Swindon!"

"God, no!" agreed Scott.

## Chapter Two

Glen Ashton, present Duke of Somerset, took his fence flying, landed in the open field that would take him back to the Somerset stables, and brought his large black gelding to a halt. He sat his horse well, with his wide shoulders nicely laid back. He was the very broth of a man at nine and twenty. Tall, athletic in build, handsome in face. His thick, silky waves of silver-laced ginger hair blew freely in the wind. His darker brows were just slightly winged over heavily lashed deep green eyes. His mouth was firm and sensuous, and he had broken hearts in his time.

He stopped and surveyed the land, now his land. Here he was, Duke of Somerset. He had never wanted it, never needed it, and here it was, all on his shoulders. His cousins were both lost at Waterloo only last year, and his uncle, their father, had died two months ago. Now all this was his. He sighed with heartfelt sadness. His uncle and cousins had been beloved intimates. They were gone . . . such a final thing. He moved his large black forward toward the Somerset Castle.

He could see the turrets in the distance. Regal and

bursting with history and pride. His? He didn't want it. His had been a very merry life. He had always had just enough funds to get on with . . . just enough. Now, now he had responsibilities! He groaned out loud. At the house now was his late uncle's solicitor and his older sister, Daphne. Damn, but he didn't feel like facing either one of them. They were filled with a strict sense of propriety, ever ready with a list of what he must and must not do.

Again the audible sigh was heard by his horse, who flicked his ears in response and wondered what his master was at.

"Well, Tim . . . what now?" Glen Ashton, present Duke of Somerset inquired of his steed. "What say you? Do I fall in and face the music?"

In answer his horse snorted, and Glen Ashton laughed. "Aye. You want your stall, your hay, and your water. What do you care for my afternoon?"

Lady Daphne Waverly was five and thirty, plump, pretty, and presently nervously wringing her dainty fingers together. She was at Somerset for the express purpose of seeing that her dear brother attend to family matters. He had shamefully neglected all his new duties in his first two months of mourning their uncle's death, but this had gone on too long. She patted her short ginger curls and turned away from the study's lead-paned glass doors to survey the little gray-haired gentleman she had known all her life, Mr. Curtis. He had been their late uncle's favorite solicitor in the firm of Curtis, Jeffry and Mettles. She could see from the way he was pursing his thin lips that he was displeased. She offered apologetically, "Glen should be back momentarily."

"Indeed," replied Mr. Curtis uncompromisingly. "His Grace was expecting me at eleven o'clock, and it is ten minutes past already."

Lady Daphne sighed and wished for the hundredth time that morning that her husband Freddy were present. Freddy always knew just what to say and . . . but she was spared the necessity of a reply when the study door opened and his Grace strode forcefully into the richly furnished, small, and cozy room.

"Ah . . . ," said the young duke softly, "Mr. Curtis, please forgive my tardiness." He smiled with the charm that had too often seen him safely out of a scrape, and its power was felt even by the stern-natured Mr. Curtis.

He eyed the new duke and could not help but be pleased. He was a man's man, handsome with ruggedness to offset the elegance of his style. He was tall, a Corinthian, and yet one could not mistake the breeding, the grace of his movements. He was arrogant, sure of himself, but with a boyish magnetism that drew one to him. Yes, thought the old solicitor, well satisfied, the title was not wasted on this one. He allowed himself a slight cough, he shifted his papers, and then he removed his spectacles to look straight into Glen Ashton's deep green eyes.

"You know, your Grace, why I am here?" He put up his hand, for he didn't want a reply. "Why your sister is here . . . what is no longer possible for you to put off?"

"Yes, but . . ." started his Grace shamelessly. What they were asking was more than he was willing to understand. They were asking him to do the impossible . . . at least it was impossible for him!

Mr. Curtis interrupted. "No, Glen. . . ." He took

the liberty of age and the years of friendship. "This time there can be no 'buts.' This is your duty to your uncle's memory!"

Ah, thought Daphne, watching quietly. Mr. Curtis just might succeed where she had failed, for he had drawn on Glen's sense of loyalty. But then she saw her brother withdraw inwardly and silently said, Oh-oh. She saw his deep green eyes take on a steely expression. She heard him speak words that were rough-edged but controlled. "And what do I owe my uncle's memory that I have neglected?" asked the Duke of Somerset between teeth that were gritted.

"I have spoken to you about this matter once before. Can it be that you did not fully comprehend the situation?" Mr. Curtis was shocked.

The Duke relaxed a little and waved this off somewhere in his sister's direction. "When we discussed it, I advised you that m'sister would be more than willing to attend to the matter for me. . . ."

"I am afraid that the law will not allow it. Your uncle specifically passed on the guardianship of his ward to you!" Mr. Curtis's face was most stern as he withdrew a letter and shoved it across the desk. "If your Grace will but read this, it may explain, for it was written to me just one day before your uncle . . . passed on."

Reluctantly Glen Ashton took up the ivory sheet of paper to read:

*Dearest Curtis:*
  *See to this for me. My ward, Felicia Easton, runs wild, I am told. I have been deceived and thought her properly supervised at her Easton*

10

*Manor home. My body will no longer serve my mind.*

*Glen has been on the town too long. He needs some settling, and though I know with a crook of the finger the boy would attend me, I'd rather he did it from his own sense of duty.*

*I leave the delicate handling of this matter in your very capable hands.*

*Arthur,*
*Duke of Somerset*

Glen Ashton's jaw pulsated as he gritted his teeth and composed himself. He looked across at the elderly man and inquired with some restraint, "Why, Curtis, did you not bring this matter to my attention earlier?"

The lawyer shook his head sadly. "I don't know how it happened, but this went first to our London offices and was set aside for me there. They thought, you see, that I would attend to my mail on one of my weekly visits to town. Your uncle's death was a source of great . . . great sadness to me as well as to you, my boy, and I did not travel to London until last week . . . at which time I did send you notice about your late uncle's ward."

"Oh, Glen," Lady Daphne moaned, "that poor child. How could you have just shelved the matter?"

He frowned. "Daffy . . . I did not . . . well, what I mean is . . . I didn't realize . . ."

"What you mean is, you did not read Curtis's letter!" snapped his sister.

If Glen Ashton were not past blushing, he would have done so now. Instead he took refuge in haughty superiority. "I *did* have other matters to attend to, after all. Now, if you will, Daff, we may settle this once and for all."

"If *I* will? Whatever do you mean?" She was struck with sudden instinctive terror. She knew her younger brother all too well. She had had the caring, the loving, and very nearly the raising of him when their parents had been killed twenty years ago. He had learned to rely on her, and it was something she had taught him. This, however, was different. He was nine and twenty. He was the Duke of Somerset and it was time he took on his life and made something of it!

"Daff . . . ," he said coaxingly, "you can't expect the poor child to go off with me alone?"

Reluctantly, she agreed that he had a point in this. "Yes, well . . . you can hire a governess or some such creature."

"Can't do that," Curtis stuck in. "Chit is too old for a governess. Twenty years, you know."

"Twenty?" This from both the duke and his sister.

"Aye," said Curtis blandly, "and running wild. Time she was brought to London . . . properly presented as your uncle would have liked her to be . . . Almack's . . . balls . . . you know . . ."

"No, I don't know," said the Present Duke of Somerset. "What in blazes am I do do with a twenty-year-old chit?" He looked at his sister. "That settles it, Daff . . . give her to you."

Horrified, Lady Daphne balked. "Give her to me? Oh, no, you do not! I will not be made a matron before my time!"

"I would imagine you might stand . . . not a matron, but a friend," said Curtis softly. "You have

12

youth enough, my lady, to make her comfortable, and from what I am told, social ton enough to give her the entrée to society.''

"Yes, well . . .'' Lady Daphne made an attempt—feeble before their peering eyes—to extricate herself. "That may be . . . but, but . . . I don't see that this is *my* responsibility. And besides, I don't want some pretty young thing bouncing around my house for my Freddy to be ogling!''

The duke laughed out loud and put a comforting arm about her. "Freddy adores you, sis. Doesn't have eyes for any other woman.''

She pouted prettily. "Maybe . . . but he *is* a man . . . and I don't think I should tempt him in our own home.''

"You won't have to," said Curtis, again softly, almost insiduously. "The Easton chit is the duke's responsibility. His ward. She should reside in his town house, properly chaperoned with a duenna. You would just be on hand to take her about.''

Lady Daphne was woman enough to be leery about having some young thing outshine her but sweet-natured enough to put this aside. She relented with a sigh. "Oh, well . . . I suppose that would be acceptable.''

"Acceptable? Not at all! Mine is a bachelor residence! It wouldn't be the thing for a twenty-year-old female to take up a living with me.''

"Yours, Duke, is the Somerset Town House in Kensington Square. It has never been and I hope will never be . . . er, bachelor lodgings. I have already sent for your cousin Amelia. She was not doing well in Bath, and I am certain she will enjoy playing

13

duenna for this ward of yours." Curtis could be most forceful in his gentle manner.

"Cousin Amelia?" The Duke was nearly choking. "Egad, Curtis, the poor woman is nearly seventy! Am I to be saddled with a foundering old woman and a squeaking twenty-year-old?"

"Yes, but Glen," stuck in his sister gently, "you have always liked poor old cousin Amelia, and we have both felt sorry for her situation. This would be just the thing for her."

"Of course it would, and no doubt it will be just the thing for little Miss Easton, but it is not . . . most definitely *not* the thing for me!"

# Chapter Three

It was six in the morning. There was a low, thick mist covering the open field. It formed waves and patterns over the tall grass and wildflowers. The huntsman in his traditional scarlet coat put up his horn and encouraged his hounds in their exercise. They were a lovely pack of black-and-tan foxhounds and they seemed intent on work. Soon the cubbing season would begin and they would be asked to show their merit.

Felicia loved watching them. It was invigorating to ride out with Huntsman Danbury and his pack. They looked liked something caught in time there in the morning mist, their noses to the ground, their ears alert for instructions. She hugged her dark brown velvet hacking jacket to herself, for there was a morning chill to the air. She patted her matching brown velvet top hat so that it was just a bit too low on her forehead, and she had to peep up to have a look at the rising slope of brush and grass. Her gray eyes twinkled as she watched the favorite of her hounds, Cardigan, seriously working when he stopped to consider another hound who had sniffed, put up his head, and howled with sheer delight. Cardigan gave the hound and the ground a moment's attention and then with an indignant sniff returned his nose elsewhere. It was obvious to him that his fellow hound was something of a fool!

Felicia giggled. "That Doobie is turning out to be a babbler, but good old Cardigan knows better than to pay him any mind."

Scott grunted in agreement to this and added, "Thing is . . . too many babblers. They'll have to be weeded out before the season begins." He sighed heavily, for they hadn't had much exercise and he was tired of keeping his horse champing at the bit. He and his animal wanted a run and he was getting bored. "Dull morning, this."

"Hmmm. Bad scenting . . . there is never any understanding it, but never mind, I will race you back to the manor and winner gets to rest back in Cook's easy chair while the loser puts together a hearty breakfast." She was glittering naughtily.

"Done!"

"Oh, I can see you think you will out do me, but you just might be wrong. Signal to Huntsman Danbury that we mean to leave. He is just hacking them back anyway."

She watched only long enough to see that the huntsman was properly notified of their intentions, then she quietly urged her gelding forward and began trotting him off and toward the field line fence. The excitement of serving Scott a trick made her giggle out loud, and he turned about in time to observe her. With a sudden dawning he realized she had already started the race and had a good distance between them.

"Little vixen!" he called after her and let his horse out.

They laughed in unison as Flip took her fence flying with more bravado than grace and Scott followed her with some show of enthusiasm. It wasn't long before they had the manor stables in view, but their youthful carefree merriment was short-lived. A young urchin whose mother worked as cook up at the house came running out to meet them, and as he held Flip's horse he blurted out portentously, "Miss . . . oi been woiting on ye this 'alf 'hour 'n' more. Somethin' terrible 'as 'appened!"

"Whatever is wrong? What do you mean?" Her fine brows drew together over her gray eyes as she considered him.

"It's the dook! They saw 'im, they did, down at Northport Village. They say 'is carriage 'as lost a wheel . . . yesterday it did . . . and it won't be ready to move for some hours yet, but . . ."

"The duke? The Duke of Somerset?" she cried in distress. "As close as Northport? Oh, no . . . oh . . ." She turned to Scott. "Scott. Scott . . . he is coming for me!"

All Scott's upbringing and breeding had prepared him for just such a moment. She was his friend, and rarely did he even think of her as female. However, at the moment she presented a damsel in distress and chivalry was clearly called for. He patted her shoulder and advised her gravely, "Never you mind. Know just what to do!"

Her gray eyes opened wide. "You do?"

"Aye," he answered and waved the urchin off. The boy left with some reluctance, for he was as interested as Flip to discover what plan young Master

17

Scott had in mind. "Take you to m'aunt's in London. Don't know why I didn't think of it sooner." At the back of his mind a doubt flickered as he thought of this particular relation.

"Your aunt? Do you mean your aunt Matilda?" Felicia shrieked in some surprise. She had on many occasions been a guest at Scott's home when his aunt Matilda had been visiting. She conjured up a mental picture of herself standing before this older woman and gulped.

"Hmmm. Only aunt in London, you know," he added thoughtfully.

Felicia frowned over this. There was Aunt Matilda in London or the duke and some outlandishly desperate place God only knew where. There wasn't really a choice. Aunt Matilda won hands down. There, she could hide herself from the oppressive duke until she came of age and had control of her money and her estate. Even so, there were realities to be thought of.

"Yes, that is, I suppose, a solution, but Scott . . . how will I get to London? Anyone who knows will tell the duke and he will come after me."

He puzzled over this for a long moment. The problem lay in the fact that he would have to come up with some viable excuse to give his father. He couldn't tell him where he was taking Flip, for his father would then be obliged to disclose the information to her legal guardian. He couldn't worry him, either, by allowing him to believe she had run off unprotected. Dawning lit up his pale blue eyes.

"Got it." With this statement he took her arm and led her toward the house.

"Do you?" She still had her doubts. "Well . . . I

don't know how and what your aunt Matilda will say when we show up at her door.''

''Never mind that now. First things first,'' answered Scott, growing into manhood with his new-found responsibility!

In Northport Village, at a quaint and properly serviced inn, Lady Daphne Waverly stomped about in her charmingly decorated bedchamber and advised her middle-aged, placid-tempered maid that her brother the duke was a villain of some stature.

''For wouldn't you know he would send me off in a Somerset coach that was too decrepit to make the journey!'' She folded her arms across her ample bosom and seethed. ''Does he accompany me? Oh, no . . . off he goes to London on some last-minute nonsense while he sends me to do his work for him! Well . . . when next I see him, he shall answer for this!''

''I am very sure he will, my lady,'' answered her maid with a certain twinkle, for she was well acquainted with her ladyship's brother.

Lady Daphne eyed her suspiciously for a moment but continued in this vein for some moments before she allowed herself to sit and sip the tea her maid had poured for her refreshment.

''Is the coach nearly ready, do you think?'' her Ladyship asked after the soothing brew had found its way to her lips.

''I will go and see, my lady.'' Her maid started for the door.

''No, no, love. Don't bother. I am certain they will send us word as soon as we can leave. Faith, but I wish I had never given in to his miserable smile!''

''Yes, my lady.''

Little did his Grace know of his sister's fit of temper in his regard as he tooled his perfectly matched pair of bay geldings down the Post Road. London was left at his broad back, and ahead, ahead lay some countrified twenty-year-old child! Egad! Whatever would he do with her?

There were, of course, several solutions, but there were also his uncle's wishes, and he found he could not easily put those wishes aside. The chit had been his uncle's ward and he must do right by her. So be it!

So be it, indeed! Whatever Curtis may say, he was a bachelor, in his thirtieth year. He was used to gadding about, used to having his friends drop by at any hour, used to . . . a great many things he would certainly have to tone down if he was to take up residence in the Somerset Town House with this child. This was impossible. He had never expected to be duke. His uncle, his cousins had been before him. He had been happy with his independence, his moderate income, indeed his life. Now he was the Duke of Somerset. Hell and fire!

It was a good four hours to Easton, and he did it in slow stages, for he didn't mean to change his horses at a posting house but to make the journey in one day, remain at Easton Manor the night, and return to London late the next morning. With any good luck Daffy had reached the manor yesterday afternoon as planned and perhaps a rapport had been established between the two females. Damn, but he hoped so. Then Daff might take the chit under her wing and he could be done with the whole mess!

# Chapter Four

"Scott, are you sure this is the correct road?" Felicia peered through the dark of the night, squinting.

He sighed and didn't bother looking back at her as he urged his horse forward. It was already past seven o'clock. They had gotten a later start than they had planned and he was desperately worried. He had to get Flip to Waterbury Inn before the hour grew much later if he was going to maintain any semblance of propriety. At least then they could pose the picture of brother and sister traveling to London together. If they arrived much later than eight o'clock, however, people would raise a brow and wonder why they were traveling at such a questionable hour on horseback. Zounds! That was just what he wanted to avoid . . . curious people. Therefore, when he finally answered her, his tone was rather testy.

"Deuce take it, girl, I have already told you that I am sure about the road. Read the fingerpost two miles back and this is the Post Road, which will eventually take us right into London." He frowned. "However, what we want now is the Waterbury Inn, and if we don't pick up the pace, we won't get there for another hour or more!''

She sniffed and refrained from sticking out her tongue at him, which is what she usually did when he spoke in such a tone. After all, he was doing all this just for her. ''Yes, well, I can't see a thing and don't want to land poor Gem here into a hole.''

''Hen-witted and chicken-hearted!'' Scott laughed. ''Any ninny can see that the road is as smooth as silk!''

Her resolve to treat him with respect was lost somewhere in the night. ''Hen-witted? Oaf! Dolt! You are naught but . . . but . . . a man much like all your kind!''

He knew her too well to be offended at such abuse. ''Like all my kind?'' he scoffed. ''And how would you know? You don't know very many men.''

''Oh, is that so? Well, you are very wrong indeed. I know quite a few. In fact . . . Daniel Waters, whom you call a top sawyer . . .''

''Danny? I introduced you to Danny.'' He was frowning. As he recalled he had specifically warned this particular friend off Felicia. Danny had been down to visit him over the holidays, and Danny had always been something of a rakehell with females. ''He didn't give you more than a glance.'' He was thinking hard, trying to recall if this were true. ''You were too much of a babe for him to bother about.''

''Is that so? Well, then, explain why he was forever trying to put his arms about me. Explain why he tried to kiss me under the mistletoe.''

Scott showed signs of severe palpitations. ''He didn't!''

"He did, and in fact I let him kiss me the second time he tried and it was rather . . . interesting."

"Flip!" Indeed, poor Scott was very much shocked. "I can't believe it."

Being female, being still insecure about herself, she puzzled up doubtfully. "Why, Scott? Don't you think me pretty?"

He hadn't the patience. "What has that to do with it? Deuce take it, girl, I told him to treat you as though you were m'own sister!" He shook his head over the matter. "Here is my closest friend down from Eton and what does he do but seduce you when my back is turned!"

"He didn't quite seduce me," Felicia offered dryly.

"No? Well, that is very nice to know, but the thing is I told him to treat you as though you were m'sister! Hands off, that means." He eyed her through the night's dusk. "And what about you? That's right! Shouldn't be letting men kiss you under the mistletoe!"

"Oh?" She dimpled naughtily. "Where should I let them kiss me?"

"Flip!" he reprimanded her in severe tones. "Don't be sassy!"

She sighed loudly. "I suppose so, but one must accumulate some experiences, after all." She thought about this and decided to give over yet another confidence. "Know what else, Scott?"

"What?" he asked cautiously.

"Thomas Brookes kissed me last month."

"Thomas?" Scott shrieked in shocked accents. "Thomas Brookes? Felicia . . . Thomas is . . . why . . . Thomas is nearly thirty-five! How dare he? How could he? Why . . . he is an old man!"

She wrinkled her nose at him. "Old? I don't think Thomas is old. He is *older*, but not old . . . and so . . . sophisticated." She sighed audibly over the experience. "It was ever so pleasant, much nicer than Danny's kiss."

"Flip! Flip . . . you can't go about letting every man in the county kiss you!" Scott's sense of propriety was deeply affected.

"Yes, well . . . he caught me by surprise . . . and besides, I felt sorry for him."

"You . . . you felt sorry for him?" Scott was now nearly beside himself.

"Indeed. He had asked me to marry him, you see . . . and I . . . said no."

"You said no, but you kissed him?" Scott demanded in strong accents of disapproval, and then added as an after thought, "Didn't know Brookes was calling on you."

"No? Well, he has been. We ride together from time to time and . . . well, I like him, but not enough to marry him. And the kiss was . . . just a parting thing, you know?"

Scott was silenced by this last and mulled it over in his mind. He answered finally, "Still, mustn't go about kissing everyone . . . understand?"

"Hmmm. I know that, silly." She looked at him for a thoughtful moment. "Funny . . ."

"Funny? What is funny?"

"Never wanted to kiss *you*. Thought about it . . . but set it aside at once."

He pulled himself up straight and his tone indicated that he had taken offense. "Oh, really? Well, there are a great many girls that have wanted to kiss me!"

She gurgled enthusiastically, as her remark had been designed to this end. "Ha! Who?"

"Mary Wiggens for one!" he spat at her and then blushed in the darkness.

There was no time for exchange of further confidences, for at this juncture a shot rang out forcefully in the night and they came to an immediate and abrupt halt.

"What the deuce . . . ?" he breathed in a hushed voice.

Instinct moved Flip. "That was a gunshot, Scotty. Let's get off the road." And when he didn't move, "Scott . . . please?"

However, he did not obey her summons, for another shot reverberated with sudden impact through the air. He spurred his horse forward with, "Damn if someone isn't in trouble!" So shouting, he moved into the darkness and was off, leaving Felicia at his back.

Flip was a stout-hearted female, but she was also made of practical stuff. Running one's horse and oneself willy-nilly to the rescue was not exactly how she would have handled the situation had she been consulted. Thus, with an unladylike oath, she too spurred her horse forward and after Scott, if only, she told herself, to stop him from getting hurt.

"Scott!" she shouted after him in some exasperation. "Scott, will you hold a moment?"

He didn't hear her, and there was nothing in his demeanor to suggest that he would have complied with her request had he heard her call. Shots blasting on the open road in the dark of night could only mean one thing to a young man ready for adventure. Highwaymen! At last, he was going to see a highwayman for himself. How many times had he heard his father and his father's friends talk about the high toby? His father had even confided that on one occasion he had been forced to kill one of these brutes to protect a young woman's honor. These men, Scott's father had taught him, were the worst kind of criminal, sneaking about in the dark, attacking women and invalids on the King's road! They should, Scott's father had proclaimed, every last one, be put to the dust!

Thus it was that Scott charged down upon what looked to be a highwayman in action. There was a coach and four ill-matched but quiet horses at a standstill. The driver of the vehicle had his hands up and was reciting in frightened accents that he was unarmed. Within the coach there was an elderly gentleman, at the moment very much in his cups and totally unaware of the proceedings around him, for he lay in something of a stupor, loudly snoring into the squabs of his leather upholstery.

This particular high toby had little skill, less fame, and a sure fear of being put in the gaol. He heard the sound of a horse fast approaching and looked around to see that some young man meant to say him nay. He called out a warning, and when this was not obeyed, he followed it up with a threat. Still, the young man bent on rescue charged his horse forward, and the irritated high toby released a shot for effect. He was never good with his pistols. He never made his mark, and he was more than a little surprised to find that he had done so now. With an oath and a spur he turned his horse sharply and fled. Damn if he wasn't in for it now! All he could think was to get away.

The driver of the coach felt much the same. He took up his whip, and with bold encouragement to his horses, spanked them forward. There were too many bullets flying for his comfort, he decided, and besides, his first duty was to get his employer home safely.

Scott's initial reaction to the sure knowledge that a bullet had pierced his flesh was total shock. Youth is such that it rarely thinks of death. His hand went to his upper chest now, and he found his fingers laden with his own warm, sticky blood. His horse was still moving at something of a pace, and without caution he attempted to rein in his animal. The effort cost him. A searing bolt of pain shot through him and exploded through his brain until his cry of anguish ended in unconsciousness. Slowly but with something of a heavy thud, he rolled off his horse and hit ground!

Felicia heard the third shot fired and arrived to find Scott tumbling to earth. With a sudden fear gripping her young heart, she nimbly jumped off her horse, and pulling it along by its reins, pounced on Scott's limp body to cry, "Scott! Oh, God . . . Scott . . . don't be dead!" His face was hidden from her, so she moved to roll him round and her hand discovered the blood staining his coat. It served to frenzy her. "Oh, faith . . . oh, Scott!"

Think, she told herself. Get yourself together and think! Here was Scott, wounded, bleeding profusely . . . perhaps . . . no, not dying! She wouldn't, couldn't let him die. He looked so white in the bleak night's darkness. What to do? Oh, faith . . . just what could she do? His horse? Where was his horse? Deuce take the beast for running off! If only she could rouse him, get him on her horse and then perhaps to help. . . .

With this last thought, she called his name again. "Scott! Scott . . . please . . . answer me . . . for me . . . open your eyes . . . Scott, you have to open your eyes . . . hear me." Naught. He just did not move a muscle, did not make a sound. She had a sudden impulse to cry. What good would it do? She had to keep her head. She had to think of something.

# Chapter Five

The errant Duke of Somerset blinked, squinted, and blinked again as he wielded his very fine pair of bays through the night. Seeing was, he thought, a difficult thing after the quantity of brandy he had consumed. He hadn't intended to linger so long at that last posting house, but then in came his cronies on their way back to London from a sporting event. One thing led to another until he had taken too much brandy and wasted too much time. Daffy, he warned himself silently, was going to be furious with him!

The road was just barely visible in the distance, for there was something of a moon and the sky was clear. However, it took some skill in the next few moments to maintain control over his high-spirited horses. A team of four and a coach, driven by a man intent on leaving a devil behind, appeared suddenly and spooked the duke's bays. They attempted to rear, but the duke brought them under control and managed to tool them out of the way. This was not easy, for the coach was an old and large vehicle whose driver bullied past.

The duke released a string of interesting curses,

brought his horses back in hand, and proceeded on, for there didn't seem to be much more he could do. He was mumbling to himself and mulling over a letter he might send off to the proper authorities when another incident occurred that put the coach and four completely out of his mind.

Felicia heard the sound of horse's hooves meeting forcefully with gravel and stone. She heard the sound of carriage wheels and all at once came to life. She could see very little of the road ahead, as it was winding and obscured by overhanging trees. However, her good sense told her that help was at hand if she moved quickly. Help for Scott. It was all she could think of obtaining, and therefore she moved with more speed than caution.

The duke's horses saw something in the distance. Its shape was not clear but it was flinging its arms in the air, and *that* was something they determined was a sure sign of impending danger. For the second time that night these poor creatures tried to go into the air, with frightened snorts and flaying hooves!

Flip tripped on a protruding rock, attempted to catch her balance, and instead landed herself neatly crumpled on the road. The duke, still fogged by brandy, but nonetheless remarkably in control and somewhat agile still, brought his horses under control. This done, he braked his open curricle, set aside his driving reins, jumped nimbly to earth, and moved to his horses' heads. Here he took a moment to pat their necks and assure himself that they were steady, and then did he move in on the cause of this last commotion!

"What the bloody hell do you think you are doing, child?" he demanded in indignant accents.

A lesser girl might have been reduced to tears. Flip was apologetic, for she had not meant to spook his fine horses and sincerely hoped they had not taken any injury.

"I *am* sorry . . . but . . ."

"But?" He was moved to outrage for she was so calm. He bent, took up both her elbows from beneath her cloak, and raised her to her feet.

She could not say why, but she found herself blushing hotly, and he unsteadied her so that she stumbled and found herself falling into his arms. There caught, she found herself a prisoner while he further assessed the situation.

Here was no child! With her body pressed up against his own, he discovered a woman. He looked closer and found long black silky hair with gleam enough to catch his eye with interest, and his tone changed when next he spoke.

"As you were saying, my love? But . . . ?"

She lowered her eyes to the ground as she gently pulled out of his hold. For some odd reason she did not want to meet his gaze. Now, what had she been saying? Faith! Scott! "Yes, please, sir . . . I . . . we . . . need your help."

"Indeed?" His brow was up for now he was intrigued.

"My brother—" she freely invented— "has been shot. I can't lift him to his horse, and he is bleeding to death on the open road!"

The duke was moved to action. He ushered her along to his open curricle, taking over the situation in his habitual authoritative style. He had her waist in his two hands, and all at once she found herself raised and planted on the curricle's well-sprung plush

31

leather bench. He jumped up beside her, and she moved over to give him more room as he reached for the driving reins.

He eyed her consideringly before he released the brake and encouraged his horses forward, asking only, "How far up the road?"

She peered through the darkness, and then when, some twenty seconds later, she saw Scott's limp form, she pointed agitatedly. "There!"

He was reining in his team, braking once more before he alighted and went to the boy. Flip hurried to follow but found her skirts a nuisance as she clambered down from the curricle and went to Scott. She watched as the duke examined Scott with a gentleness that surprised her. He was so large, so commanding that she had rather thought he hadn't it in him to be gentle.

"He needs attention at once," the duke said, attempting to advise her of the situation, yet restraining his tones in order to keep her from becoming further alarmed over her brother.

"Yes, for faith's sake!" she uttered with some impatience. "That is what I told you."

"We'll put him in the curricle," returned the Duke thoughtfully. "How far is your home from here?"

"No . . . no . . . we don't live nearby. . . ." Flip was frowning.

The Duke's brow went up. "Don't you?" Then because there wasn't time to discuss this now, "Very well . . . we'll have to go to the Andover Inn."

"Yes, but that is ten minutes down the road," Felicia worried out loud.

"So it is, but we haven't a choice," he said grimly. He was bending once more over Scott. "Go on, girl.

Take up his feet and be as gentle as you can. We'll have to manage him on the curricle."

Some moments later, this was done, Scott's horse was found and tethered at the curricle's rear, and Flip was on her horse once more, following as the duke led them to the Andover Inn. She watched his back as he worked his horses and steadied Scott, who had been drifting in and out of consciousness. An unusual man, this, with such an air! Conceited, too . . . and arrogant. She wasn't quite sure she liked him.

However, thirty minutes later, Flip had cause to be grateful for the stranger's arrogance, self-assurance, and air of command. She watched him handle the innkeeper and the innkeeper's staff with considerable style. In a thrice, a groom had been sent to fetch the doctor. A very acceptable room had been prepared, a fire lit in its small but adequate grate, and Scott neatly deposited between clean sheets in a large four-poster bed.

The innkeeper's small, thin wife fluttered into the room with a pitcher of hot water and a wad of clean strips for bandages. She bustled for a moment, declared that she wasn't good about wounds and blood, excused herself, and then quickly disappeared. Scott opened his eyes again, looked up at Flip's frowning features, and attempted a smile.

"Ah, girl, I've gone and done it. Ruined all our fine plans."

She touched his wet forehead lightly with a damp rag and quieted him. "Hush, love."

"It was a highwayman, you know," he mumbled at her and then attempted to raise himself up. "Where . . . are we?"

Gently she pushed him back down and winced

when he groaned. "Oh, Scotty, stop it, please. I have to get your coat off. We are at the Andover . . . and a doctor is on his way."

"The Andover?" He was feeling light-headed from the loss of blood, but this did sink in. "How . . . how did you get me here?"

"This . . . gentleman managed it." She realized she did not even know the stranger's name. She glanced at him, for he was standing opposite her with his shoulder leaning into an oak cabinet, his arms folded across his chest. With his hat and cloak off, he looked the fashionable London rake, and she noted that he was eyeing her with some interest. She tugged at Scott's coat and was able to slip it off him, but it caused him a great deal of discomfort and he yelped at her.

"Flip!" he nearly shouted. "Will you stop fussing over me!"

"I have to clean your wound," she answered firmly.

"Well, then, do you think you could manage to do it without killing me?" He was testy.

She could see the tightness about his lip, the paleness of his cheeks, and she smiled fondly at him, touched his nose, and said. "Oh, hush, love." She tore away his shirt and bolstered herself when she saw the nastiness of the wound the bullet had left.

While she cleansed away the blood, Scott had managed to turn his head to survey the tall stranger. He smiled wearily and said, "How do you do, sir? I am Scott Hanover." He bit his lip. Perhaps he should not have divulged that piece of information.

"I do better than you at the moment, Scott Hanover." The duke smiled. "I am . . ." He hesitated only a moment before introducing himself. "Glen Ashton." He did not add that he was the Duke of Somerset. Why? He didn't want to overawe these children. Yes, here was a mystery and there was no sense clouding it up with high-sounding titles. What they might confide to a man on their level, they certainly would think to withhold from a duke!

"Well, well," said a voice from the open doorway, "so here is the boy." The doctor was a small round man with a bald head and a kind smile. He glanced at Felicia and said, "I see you have had some very good attention." He then moved in and she made room for him, watching anxiously as he bent over Scott.

The duke found Felicia beside him as she moved farther away and out of the doctor's path. She was an engaging creature, for she peeped up at him for reassurance as the doctor made some strange "ah" and "oh" sounds. He found himself taking and patting her dainty hand.

It seemed an interminable time before the doctor turned to the duke, who he assumed to be in charge of the situation, and said, "The bullet passed straight through the lad. No main arteries were severed. There is the wonder of it, but we still have to worry about infection. He has lost a great deal of blood, so I don't mean to leech him. I'll see to the dressing now and be back in the morning." He glanced at Felicia once again. "Perhaps you had better take Miss Hanover to her own room now, for I mean to give the lad something to help him sleep."

"As you wish, doctor, but when your ministrations are complete, do stop by and have a word with me. I'll be in the private parlor." So saying, the duke took up Flip's elbow and began leading her out of the room.

She made a feeble objection. "Yes, but . . ."

"No 'buts,' my girl. It is time you and I had a chat . . . and"—he smiled at her now, belying the hardness of his words with the charm of his twinkling green eyes—"a bite to eat, for I would wager you are just as hungry as I."

It occurred to her that she was famished and her gray eyes glinted appreciatively. "Yes, isn't it terrible, but I am hungry."

"Why terrible?" he frowned, and was amused.

"Because there is Scott, in bed, shot, and in an awful state, and the first moment away from him what should I do but want to gorge myself." She clucked over this fact in self-abuse.

He laughed and was moved to tweak her nose. "Well, it is perfectly natural for you to be hungry after such an adventure and *after* you have seen Scott attended to and safe."

She cocked her pretty face at him and considered this. "Hmmm. That is, I suppose, a more comfortable way of looking at it."

They had by this time reached the private parlor the duke had hired for the evening, for he meant to find out over a substantial meal just what these two scamps were up to. That they were brother and sister he very much doubted. They were no doubt eloping, and yet there was very little of the lover in either one's carriage. Interesting.

# Chapter Six

Felicia found herself ushered into a small, cozy room. Its walls were trimmed in dark wood, with a Tudor effect. Its one window was small, square, and shuttered with a matching dark wood frame. Paintings of countryside, foxhounds, and horses ornamented the mellow pale yellow of the walls between the stripes of dark oak, and one entire wall was taken by an attractive fireplace.

The room was dimly lit with candlelight and the flame from the fire in the grate. The small round dining table was already covered and set for dinner, for two. Felicia looked at this, shyly glanced at the duke, and moved to the window seat in some sudden nervousness. She didn't know what to do with herself. Here she was in her old rough-and-tumble brown print gown with her long hair loose like a schoolgirl's, and here was this . . . this *man*! Ah, and such a man!

He sensed her sudden shyness and smiled to himself, for he was determined to draw her out. He allowed her to finger the shutters for a moment before he called her attention. "Come here and warm yourself by the fire, child."

It was gently said, but she took umbrage at his choice of words. "I am *not* a child."

He chuckled and made her a mock bow. "Oh. Are you not? Do forgive me. Come here, then. What *is* your name?"

"Hanover," she answered, but her eyes did not meet his. Felicia Hanover."

"Ah, yes. Felicia . . ." He extended his hand in a welcoming gesture.

She moved toward him and found him seating her in the large upholstered wing chair by the fire. She objected, "Oh, no . . . but where will you sit?"

"Here," he said, drawing over another, less comfortable-looking, chair.

A serving girl whose mop cap was askew and whose breath was labored from all the sudden work she had been given entered the room at that moment and plopped a basket on the table announcing, " 'ere are rolls and breadsticks . . . hot fresh from the oven."

The duke thanked her, watched her go, and turned once more to Felicia. He took but one moment and said, "Felicia, is it? I fancy young Scott called you something else." He waited for her to supply it.

She smiled. "Flip. He has always called me Flip."

"And do you prefer that to Felicia?"

"I am rather used to hearing it." She was about to add that she and Scott grew up together when she realized that such a statement would not do.

He got up and fetched the basket of rolls, offering her one as he pulled his chair closer to hers. He watched her select one, thinking that she was quite a taking little thing as he placed the basket on a small round serving table at his elbow. He said nothing for a moment, giving her time to nibble happily at her roll before he interrupted the peace of the moment with a question—gently, innocently put.

"Well, my pretty Felicia, what sent you and young Scott out tonight? Trouble?" His tone invited her to confide. His green eyes stroked her.

She made the mistake of looking into those eyes, for she didn't realize then just how many women had fallen beneath their spell, and she blushed. What a rush of feeling she suddenly underwent! Her first words in answer to his question were almost stammered out. "We . . . we were on our way to London." She did not look at him but gravely studied what was left of her roll and added, "This is very good. Why don't you have one while they are hot?"

He ignored this with a smile and dove in for the kill. "On your way to London? In the dead of night? Why?"

She sighed and answered honestly, "We had no choice." She couldn't be rude to him with a snub. He had helped them, he had been so very kind, and there was something about him that made her almost cower into sweet submission.

"No choice?" His tone couldn't have caressed more. "But my dear, why is that?"

She dimpled at him and went kitten-like onto her chair, tucking her legs beneath her. "Shall I trust you, sir?"

He found himself momentarily enchanted. She was a ragamuffin of a child, nothing more, yet her lips were pursed, cherry-red and enticing. Her form was trim, yet provocatively alluring. Her hair unfashionably long, but ever so thick, black and beckoning with its shine. He had a sudden urge to reach over and brush away a stray strand from her shoulder. Could she trust him? This was something new. Whenever a woman had asked such a question before, he had honestly replied in the negative. He said gravely, "Indeed, my imp, you may."

"We . . . were running away . . ." she confided in a hushed tone.

"Running away?" He repeated the words only as encouragement for her to proceed with the rest of her story, for this in no way surprised him. "From whom? Your parents?"

She blushed again, for she found it difficult to lie to him, and now she would have to if he was going to insist on details. She couldn't tell him the whole story. He might find it the ethical thing to advise her guardian of her whereabouts. So with something of a sad sigh she fabricated half-truths into a gothic tale. "I have a very old, very unfeeling guardian. My father died, and then my stepmother, you see . . . and he took over my estate and now means me to marry his son . . . to get my money, you see."

"Felicia, he cannot force you to the altar with anyone," offered the duke on a frown. "Who is this guardian of yours?"

Faith! Now what? He wanted a name. She gulped and said, "The Earl of Paddington." Thus giving him substance, she searched her mind, hoping the name was but a creation and that no "real" earl would appear to claim his title.

The duke puzzled over this name, for he had never heard it before. However, there were impoverished Irish noblemen about that he would not be aware of, so he put this aside and proceeded. "He wishes to give you a title . . . and his son an estate, is that it?"

She nodded silently and avoided his deep green eyes. How dreadful you are, she told herself, lying to him . . . to this wonderful man.

He played with his lower lip a moment and said gently, "It is often done, my dear. Marriages of convenience are a way of life among the beau monde."

"Then I don't wish to be a part of the beau monde!" she returned with enthusiasm, for here was a subject she could expound upon. "When I marry, it will be for love!"

He smiled indulgently. When he had been her age, he thought that he would do so, marry for love. However, that had been a dream which had turned into a nightmare. The girl of his heart had other . . . richer plans. He knew better now. Love was just a word. "Ah . . . so that is it. Love, eh? You and young Scott?"

She pulled a grimace at him. "That is a very silly notion. I would have expected it from another, but *not* from you. Anyone should be able to see that I love Scott, but as a sister, so that was not completely a lie, you see. We have been brought up in one another's way, and it was only natural that Scott should want to save me."

"How did he mean to do this?" The duke shook his head. "Running off with you in the middle of the night is not the answer."

"Oh, yes it is. We have a plan," she said on a superior note.

"A plan?" He smirked on purpose to draw her out, for she looked as though she was going to return her attention to the roll and button up. "Like getting shot and ending up here?" It was a taunt.

It worked. She fired up. "That was unfortunate.

41

Such things happen, you know. One cannot predict everything.'' She sighed over the night's events. ''Scott will be better presently and then we shall go to London.''

''For what purpose?''

''Scott has an aunt. He means to take me there, where I can hide from my guardian until I come of age . . . which is not so very far off. Two more months.''

It was said with such yearning that he could not stop himself from bending toward her and tweaking her nose. He chuckled then and looked up, for a serving girl had appeared with a tray laden with their substantial dinners.

''Well, for now, infant, let us attend to our dinner.''

''Hmmmm,'' agreed Felicia.

# Chapter Seven

Felicia pushed away her dish of apple pie and exclaimed that she couldn't eat another bite, with which she sighed contentedly and got up from the table.

The duke chuckled and watched her now as she meandered about the room. He took in the shape of her profile as she perused the cover of an aged volume of literature, smiled at her as she addressed some casual remark his way concerning the volume. This was a momentary diversion—this girl, the boy abovestairs. Their plight had waylaid him from his purpose. He was due to meet his sister and take charge of his ward! Due? Zounds, he exclaimed to himself, he was quite overdue. There was no doubt that Daffy would be ready to kill when next she met him. However, there was nothing for it. He could not strand these plucky children. He couldn't leave them to their own devices. Why, just look at what had become of them on their first undertaking!

"What are you thinking?" Felicia inquired of him with a tilt of her pretty head. "You look so very . . . upset."

"I was wondering what I was going to do with you . . . and Scott," he answered her honestly.

Felicia's independence came rushing to her lips. "It is not your place, sir, to *do* anything with us!" And then quickly, because she was aware of how rude she must have sounded, she added, "We . . . we are quite capable of taking care of ourselves."

He was just a trifle angered and it was displayed in the sharpness of his tone. "As you have so adequately demonstrated!"

She blushed and bit her lip. "Accidents can happen to anyone."

"Especially when one rushes headstrong into them," he retorted.

She gave him her back and moved to the fireplace, where she took up the poker and played with the logs.

"The fire burns well enough," he said after a moment as though to make peace. "Come, Felicia. We have to talk."

She turned and eyed him doubtfully. "Not if you mean to be disagreeable."

He smiled at that. "Well, I don't." He got up from the table with his hand outstretched for hers.

Oddly enough, it seemed the most natural thing in the world to give him her hand, and when he took it, he put it up to his lips and said softly, "There, my pretty little thing, I did not mean to offend."

She found herself preening beneath the weight of his compliment, blushing before the charm of his engaging smile, and she discovered a sudden uncharacteristic sense of inadequacy. She allowed him to guide her to the chairs they had occupied earlier by the burning fire, and as she found herself seated she concentrated her gaze on the leaping flames in the grate.

He opened the subject again. "Have you considered the fact that Scott will not be able to travel for at least a week?"

She looked up at that. "Oh . . . no . . . as much as that?"

Such desperation in those beautiful gray eyes! He could see the wheels turning in her mind. She was looking for an answer. He could withhold it. He could leave these two to themselves. After all, Daffy was awaiting him at Easton Manor. He answered gently, "As it happens, I am in no great rush to get to where I am going. I will wait out the week with you, advance you the ready for your shot here at the inn. . . ."

"No." She shook her head resolutely. "I couldn't let you do that."

"And why not? Your credit is good with me. You have said you are a lady of means." He was teasing her now.

She blushed, for while this was true enough, she couldn't allow him a week here with them. He would be sure to find out who she was, and then he would be obliged to inform her guardian. What a deuced uncomfortable situation this was!

"It wouldn't be seemly . . . it would attract undue attention to us," she offered.

"Ah. Perhaps I should announce myself as a relative . . . an uncle, perhaps?"

She grew even redder and shook her head. "No, you don't look old enough to be my uncle."

For some unaccountable reason, this pleased him. However, he pursued. "It would serve to make things a bit more comfortable for all of us and reduce the questions people might ask.''

She clenched and unclenched her hands. "A week? What if someone were to come this way? What if . . . ?''

"How far from home are you?'' he asked casually.

She could not be so easily taken in and knew better than to answer. "That doesn't matter. Someone might come searching after us.'' She got up from her chair and moved to the fire, giving him her back. "I won't be taken . . .'' She bit her lip before she said any more.

He got up and found himself putting his hands on her shoulders and turning her toward him. "Don't worry, scamp. One thing I can promise you is that no one shall make you marry when you don't wish it.''

Her gray eyes found his green and she felt her knees tremble. She had given him a lie, and now she had to live with it. He was so kind, so gallant, so wonderful, and she had lied. The knowledge made her want to cry. He saw the tears start in her eyes and suddenly was moved to hold her to him, pat her back comfortingly, and stroke her long black hair. She was a rough-and-tumble girl. She was wild, headstrong, and childlike. In fact, she was more child than woman. He had even found himself talking in a man's easy vernacular. *Pay her shot*, he had said. *Advance her the ready!* No way to speak to a lady . . . a woman? This was absurd! She was someone's legal ward. He had only her side of the story, and *that* still did not totally ring true. Yet he found he could not just desert her now.

"Come along,'' he found himself saying as he put

her away from his arms. "Time to go up, wash, and get some sleep."

She shook her head and sighed softly. "No . . . I think not."

In some reasonable exasperation, he demanded, "No? You think not?"

"I mean to sit up and watch Scott . . . in case . . ."

He waited for no more but firmly took her arm and began pulling her along toward the stairs. "You, my girl, will do exactly as I bid you and that is, for now, to get some rest!"

"Yes, but . . ." she persisted.

"If anyone is going to sit up with Scott . . . for the sake of propriety, it will be I"

She gasped. "Oh, no. I couldn't let you do that." She stopped him at the foot of the stairs by touching his hand.

He felt an electric shock go through him and he looked down at her, for he was startled by the sensation. "Little one . . . I must ask you not to argue with me. I am used to getting my own way."

She lowered her eyes and then flashed them at him with the peep of a smile. "I see," she said softly. Here, indeed, was a man! "Thank you." No one had ever managed her in just this fashion.

As she took the stairs to her room she marveled over the miracle. He spoke and she obeyed. Not only did she obey but she found a certain pleasure in it. Such a nice feeling to allow this particular man to take over. . . .

Odd, that! Felicia was herself used to getting her own way. She had ruled her father and her stepmother with pert, sassy, and adorable style. She often wielded friends with her charm, her easy manners, and her own brand of stubbornness. To be ordered about by anyone was something she had never allowed, and yet here she was, meekly going up to her room and . . . and pleased about it!

Strange. Very strange.

He watched her go up the stairs and frowned to himself. What was this? Now he had sent her off to bed and he was going to spend the night in a wing chair watching over a lad he had never known until this night! How the devil had he got himself into this situation? How the devil would he come about?

# Chapter Eight

Felicia opened her eyes with a start and sat straight up, a question hitting her hard: Where was she? She looked around and squinted against the bright rays of the sun and grimaced. She had forgotten to draw the pretty yellow hangings last evening. Last evening? Oh, faith! That was right. She was at some strange inn, with Scott wounded down the hall and a stranger looking after them! What a very odd thing indeed!

She sighed and sank back against the pillows. How good he had been, this handsome Glen Ashton. He had even ordered a hot bath drawn for her in her room. What a nice surprise that had been when she opened the door of her room last evening and found it waiting. How very sweet and thoughtful!

She glanced around the room. A charming chamber with bright yellow flowers dominating the quaint papered walls. Scott's room was . . . ? Scott! Zounds, girl! Here you are mewling over a strange man and a pretty room while Scott lies helpless in his bed. Well, not quite helpless, she answered herself. *He* had promised to look in on Scott during the night. Well, she couldn't sleep anymore. She would go have a look in on Scott.

With more haste than care, she washed, brushed her long black hair into strands of gleaming hues, tied the thick silk at the nape of her neck, and threw on her smallclothes. A moment later she was struggling into her brown paisley gown and thanking her good sense for having prompted her to choose a gown that buttoned down the front of the bodice. She pulled on her boots, took up her dark cloak, and moved to her chamber door. A quick glance down the dark corridor confirmed the belief that she was probably the only person up and about, so with some caution and several quiet steps, she made the distance to Scott's room.

Just as she took hold of the latch, the grandfather clock startled her with its chime. Six o'clock? Faith! She hadn't thought it was this early! Well, she would just have a look in on Scott and then perhaps take an early morning ride. That was what was needed.

The drapes in Scott's room were drawn, and though a small fire still burned in the grate there was very little light. She moved gingerly to the bed and looked at him for a long considering moment. He was sleeping peacefully, but she reached and felt his forehead. There didn't seem to be any heat . . . no fever. Good. Reassured, she dropped a kiss upon his cheek and made her way back to the door. She never noticed a dark figure reclining in the wing chair between the fireplace and the foot of the bed. However, the dark figure had been fully awake, and he had noticed her!

Glen Ashton watched her and restrained a groan, for he felt stiff from having been uncomfortably situated all night. He saw her sign of affection to Scott and then he watched her leave. It had been a bad night. Scott was now sleeping peacefully, but that had not been true for a good part of the night. The lad had fevered and the duke had spent some hours rubbing him down with rose water and alcohol. He had managed to bring down the boy's temperature, but it had killed all chance for sleep for himself. Now he was stiff, uncomfortable, irritable, and cursing himself for having gotten involved. What was going on? Why was the girl sneaking in to give the boy a kiss? She was fully dressed and had her cloak with her. What was the meaning of this?

Leaving? She was leaving the inn? No, impossible. She wouldn't leave Scott. Would she? Why? Where would she go? How could she? What the devil was she doing? Was she so frightened of this guardian of hers that she would leave Scott and journey to London on her own?

Damn if he was going to allow it!

It didn't take Felicia long to saddle up her horse, slip the bit in his mouth, and walk him to the mounting block, where she hoisted herself up with agility. It was a glorious morning, crisp and fresh-smelling. The stableboys had been up and about mucking out stalls, and one had hurried forward and offered to tack up her horse, but she had smiled and told him to go about his business and she would take care of hers. He had scratched his grimy face over this, for ladies of quality did not often tack up their own horses in a public stable!

Flip spied a fence line and noted the open field ahead. She hadn't worked her animal enough to take a high fence, so she looked down the line for easier access and spied a place where the top rail had come down. "Aha! Come on, then!" she said out loud and smiled to herself. This was easily trotted and her gelding took the small fence in easy stride.

She allowed him rein in the field, watching the ground for possible holes, and after coming close to one too many, she brought him in and moved toward the fence line. She took this and covered ground for the next ten minutes at a trot. Then she pulled in to a stop and gazed about. Odd, the country was subtly changing, she thought, and it would be best to keep an eye for landmarks or she might find herself lost.

It was at this moment that she heard voices, and something, her instincts no doubt, kept her very still.

"Aw, now, missy . . . ye fuss loikes this and oi'll 'ave no choice but to dim yer lights! Ye won't loike that, ye won't."

In response there was a muffled cry and the sharp snort of a horse, as though someone had just given it an unexpected kick.

"There! Ye went and dun it!" clucked the rough-voiced man. He looked around and found his comrades coming toward him and said to the still figure in the wagon at his back, "Aye . . . 'ere are the boys now . . . we'll be taking ye by 'orse the rest of the way, we will!"

Felicia was off her horse in a thrice. Something dreadful was going on. She couldn't see through the thick of the leaves, but the voice carried so well, they had to be near. If only her gelding would just keep grazing and not make any sound. She tethered his reins to a nearby branch, giving him just enough length to graze on the leaves, before she gingerly picked her way over the fence and through the thicket.

52

There she found a narrow dirt road. She looked farther and her eyes widened with surprise.

Standing on the road was a wagon pulled by a single horse and driven by one of the roughest-looking men she had even seen. Three more men arrived, these on horseback. One of them dismounted, picked up a bundle wrapped in a blanket from the back of the wagon, and slung it over the saddle on his horse. The blanket groaned in feminine resonance. Felicia's eyes widened even more.

The man driving the wagon seemed to be in charge. Felicia watched him jump down from his perch and heard him order another of his crew down from his horse, whereby he commanded in harsh accents, "Dimwits, the lot of you! 'Ave oi got to be leading ye all by yer noses?" He shook his head and continued, "Jack and me will toike 'er the rest of the way to the cabin. Ye lads get rid of the wagon, show yer faces in town, and then meet us there. Don't be dillydallying longer than ye 'ave to and don't be talking to no one, either!"

This was grumbled over but finally agreed to, and the four men split up into pairs. Felicia gulped but decided there was only one thing to do in this situation. She would follow the two men with the bundle. She waited until they had gone a distance before taking the reins of her horse and moving forward in pursuit. She could track them. The road was a hard dirt one, but the horses' shoes left clear, fresh tracks, and this was an easy enough job until she missed the turnoff. However, she backtracked and noted the disturbed section of leaves that led deeper into the woods. There she found a very narrow woodland path. She led her chestnut gelding down this route until she spied a weathered cottage in the distance. It was at this juncture that she took her horse off the path and into the woods. She found a spot where the gelding could graze and there tethered him once more. She then slunk the remainder of the way toward the cottage on her own.

She got as far as the back of the cottage and bent beneath its dirty window to listen, and what she heard made her young heart beat furiously.

"Aye, we'll come out of this wit' a pretty guinea or two, don't ye think, Jackie-boy?"

"Oi left the letter at old man Wilson's 'ouse. If 'e wants 'er back in one piece 'e'll pay, 'e will!" answered the taller man. He poured himself a tin of ale and gulped it down. "What's the mort doing, sleeping? Or did ye bump 'er one, Clemmy?"

"Aw, now . . . the mort wouldn't keep still . . . 'ad no choice . . . but lookee . . . she be coming round already."

Felicia sank to the ground and put a hand to her forehead. There was a girl in there . . . abducted by these, these dreadful men! Faith! What to do? Just as she was worrying about how to rescue the girl within, a hand moved hard into place over her mouth, and she felt her heart scream, for her mouth was incapable of making a sound! She felt herself held in a steel-like grip and she moved into position, for she would not be taken without a battle. She would kick, punch, and grapple, but, just as she made these mental plans a familiar voice whispered in her ear.

"Be still vixen . . . or they shall hear us!" It was a sharp command although softly spoken.

She relaxed in Glen Ashton's arms and her gray eyes gleamed appreciation when he allowed her room enough to turn in his hold and look at him. Still, he put a gloved finger to her lips and lightly touched them before taking her hand, urging her up and taking her along with him into the woods, out of earshot. She felt an overwhelming sensation. She knew not what it was, this sensation, but she did know she was awfully glad to find Glen Ashton here, at her side, taking over. It was such a relief!

He took up her shoulders and she looked into his deep green eyes and felt odd, but there was no time to investigate this feeling, for he was already issuing orders to her.

"I want you to ride back to the inn and have Hodgings fetch the magistrate and some help." He was moving now, toward her horse, releasing the animal's reins from the branch, taking her arms.

"Yes, but . . ." she started to object.

"Don't argue with me, woman! I haven't the time. Just do as I ask." He mitigated the harshness of his words with a caressing glance and the touch of his gloved fingers on her nose. "That's my pretty. Go on, now, but be careful when you cross the fields."

"I am always careful," she answered testily, her chin well up as he hoisted her into her saddle.

He touched her knees and tipped his hat to her. "Are you, love? Go on, then, but Felicia, you are not to do more than lead them to me here. Understood?" His tone was stern. "I will come to you. You are not to bring them to the cottage."

She started to argue this but instead held her tongue and said quietly, "Understood." This would allow her some leeway. She could understand very well, but that didn't mean she had to obey.

"That's my girl. Off with you, now." He patted

her leg and watched her ride off. This was serious business. He had followed Felicia initially because he couldn't fathom what she was about at such an early hour. By the time he had realized she was only out for a morning ride, he had heard the voices, just as she had, and he had followed her then, if only to keep her safe from harm. Now, well, now there was a child in trouble, and that drew yet another response!

# Chapter Nine

It was a frustrating business, the matter of finding and securing help. Breathless, Felicia left her horse to be walked with the stableboy as she ran to the back entrance of the inn and found Hodgings in the kitchen. In laconic and disjointed sentences, she poured out her morning's escapade, so it was not easily or speedily that Hodgings understood. Finally, dawning lit on his face, and he announced that a magistrate must be sent for.

"Yes, yes, a magistrate and his beadles," she put in hastily.

Together they composed a note of sorts and entrusted it to the groom. There was nothing left to do but wait, so Felicia took herself upstairs to wake Scott and inform him of this latest development. She found him sitting up with a scowl upon his fair face. As she walked into the room, he directed her to survey his breakfast tray and tell him, if she could, what was on it.

She was momentarily diverted and did indeed inspect the tray, only to pull a grimace, "Ugh," she remarked, "gruel." Then with a shake of her head, "But 'tis what the doctor ordered."

"Did he, by God?" returned Scott with some disgust. "Well, take it away. I want eggs and sirloin!"

"Yes, but never mind that now. Scott, the most exciting thing has happened!"

Eggs, sirloin, and gruel were forgotten as Felicia poured out her tale, embellishing it with all the descriptions a young man might appreciate, so that her friend was wide-eyed with interest. He considered her a moment when she had done and inquired, "A child, you say? How old do you think the child is?"

Felicia puzzled over this. "I don't know. I can't be certain she is a child. And if she is, she is rather tall . . . taller than I . . . or at least . . . slumped over in the blanket she looked rather long."

"She? How do you know it is female?" he asked. "Flip, are you sure this is not all a hum?"

"Why, Scott! Would I tell you some ridiculous nonsense? Whatever for?"

"To keep me from my eggs and make me eat my gruel," he returned pugnaciously.

She giggled and fluffed his hair at his forehead. "Silly brat. This is not a hum, and I really think it is a female, because I did hear it groan . . . and it sounded feminine, and though I couldn't hear everything they said, I had the notion they were talking about a female."

A knock sounded and a serving girl appeared, dropped a curtsy, and informed Felicia that "sir" was awaiting her belowstairs.

"Right," said Flip getting up, dropping a kiss on Scott's head and moving off.

"Flip!" he called after her. "Don't be getting your neck stretched."

She beamed at him. "Not to worry, love. Mr. Ashton will be there."

Scott gave her a half smile and when she had left returned his attention to the gruel. He made a disparaging sound and tugged at his bellrope. "Damn this stuff," he called out loudly, "I won't eat it!"

Glen Ashton waited in the woods as close to the cottage as he dared and wondered what in thunder he was doing there. The two men within the cottage pulled out a deck of cards and began bickering over the game that ensued. Therefore, it was with a start that Ashton found he had to dive for the very thick of the woods as the man called Jack threw his cards on the table, took up a bucket, and announced that he was going to fetch some water and cook up some stew.

"Aw, now, Jack!" complained the other. "Finish up the 'and, do. What kind of a sport be ye?"

"Oi don't give a monkey for the 'and, the sport, or nothin'. Oi be hungry and there ain't one lick in 'ere to satisfy a man."

"There be yesterday's mutton," suggested Clem.

"Know what, Clem? Ye be naught but pig-gutted, pig-headed and . . ." He didn't finish the sentence, as he had a stool flung at his head. He thwarted the blow with the side of his arm, cursed his cohort loudly, and stomped out of the cottage with the bucket in hand.

Things had happened hurriedly all morning. Glen Ashton, in his rush to follow Felicia, had taken one of the inn's saddles and thrown it on one of his carriage horses. The animal was a lovely creature, a dark bay with many outstanding qualities, including youth. A five-year-old, unused to being without his perfectly matched partner, he found himself alone in the woods. Nervously he nibbled at the leaves, attempting to comfort himself. It didn't work. Everything was strange. He whinied for his buddy back in the inn's safe barn. No answer. He looked for his human and saw only birds, rabbits, and other dangerous beasts. He wanted to go home!

It was after he made this decision that he saw a rather large being walking in his direction and carrying an ominous-looking weapon. This was more than the poor horse was willing to take. He released a snort of some resonance, hopped and reared into the air, broke his reins free of the branch that held them, and took off for almost anywhere else!

"Damn!" Glen Ashton breathed, a witness to this last.

Jack stopped in his tracks and his eyes narrowed. "What in hell . . . ?" he said out loud to himself, and then as the meaning of this suggested itself to him he glanced through the woods.

Ashton had to silence him before he alerted the man in the cottage. This would take some cat-and-mouse playing. Perhaps, just perhaps he would let the mouse come to him?

They rode at a heady pace, the magistrate, the two stout and sturdy individuals he had thought to enlist, and Felicia. They were nearly out of breath when they reached the woods, leaving the open field at their back. Felicia, in the lead, put up her hand for a silent halt. They gathered around her and she whispered, "There is a trail just within the trees, but we must be careful, for I don't know if the other two have returned yet or not."

Horse pistols were produced and brandished to Felicia's wide stare, for these men did not appear to her to know what to do with their weapons. She cautioned, "Perhaps . . . pistols will not be called for . . . ?"

The magistrate nodded and his expression was grave. "Don't you worry your pretty little head over it, my dear. We won't fire a shot unless forced to it." He turned to his two comrades and called for their opinion on the matter. "Right, lads?"

His men grunted in apparent agreement. Felicia's face told the story of her thoughts as she turned to lead them forward. Heartily she hoped they would not meet with the two men on their return. Now she peered through the woods longingly for a sign of Glen Ashton. It was then that a sound, somehow familiar, caught her attention and she stopped her horse. Something was moving toward them . . . at a desperate pace!

Ashton's horse! Felicia's gray eyes opened wide as her brain went to work. Trouble. The bay gelding had no doubt been spooked by something and perhaps had even attracted notice. Glen Ashton might be in trouble. A certain fear gripped her as she turned to explain hurriedly, "That is Mr. Ashton's horse!"

The bay stopped abruptly and snorted, his head well up. Here were people. Here were other horses and one of these horses he seemed to know. Ah, yes, it was the chestnut gelding he had spent the night with. He stood still and waited.

Felicia made soothing sounds as she went to him. He allowed her to take up his reins and lead him beside her horse. There was a certain comfort in numbers. The men at Felicia's back exchanged a few more grumbles, and one of the stout fellows expressed the view that he rather thought Felicia's Mr. Ashton might have been nabbed.

Felicia frowned at him but gave him no other response as she made her way through the woods, and then she halted with a start, for she heard the harsh report of a gun.

"Damn, if we ain't in for it now!" breathed the magistrate grimly. "Stand aside, girl . . . and then, *stay here*!"

In the meantime, the mouse had indeed come to the cat! Ashton had crackled a twig with serious purpose and waited. He had no pistol with him, but he had his stock tie neckcloth and his handkerchief. With any good luck, these might do the trick. Jack heard the crackling of the twig and took the bait. He put down his bucket and peered into the woods, took up a heavy branch, and as he moved deeper into the thicket, batted the branch menacingly into the palm of his other hand. He felt a shiver shake his spine, and then out of nowhere the very fury of a man struck with a force that sent him reeling backward!

Deftly the duke had moved into position, and when he sprang it was with both hands held together in a fist that was like an iron ball! He landed his man a heavy facer, and as Jack fell back, he was on top of him, his neckcloth nicely wrapped around Jack's wide neck. However, Jack was able to get off one desperate cry, and it was carried well with the wind. The duke choked the breath out of his man, and when Jack was nearly out, he took his handkerchief and stuffed it into Jack's mouth. Then he rolled Jack onto his belly, took his hands and tied them at Jack's back with the well-used neckcloth, and stood back to inspect his handiwork with a frown. Had Jack been heard by the man in the cottage?

Clem stood up with a start and tried to think. That was Jack. He had heard Jack cry out. What, then? What was wrong? Why wasn't Jack back yet with the water? Damn the fool! No doubt there was a simple explanation, but even so, he reached for his pistol, held it comfortingly poised in his large hands, and moved outdoors. Instinctively, he knew that trouble was lurking. He felt it rush up his spine and jangle his nerves.

"Jack . . . eh, fool . . . where be ye?" he called out in gruff tones.

He looked toward the heart of the woods. His men had not returned yet, but they would soon. There was some comfort in that, at least, so he went farther into the thicket and called again. "Dimwit! Where 'ave ye gone off to, then?" He stopped and looked around. He was still in something of a clearing. He could easily be picked off by a shot if someone had that in mind. He took another step into the woods. What to do? What to do?

This was all the duke needed to get into a position to instigate his plan. A rock carefully aimed and forcefully thrown whizzed over Clem's uncovered head. Clem was unnerved already. This last brought up his gun, and he got off a shot with more speed than thought. The duke rushed him before he had time to reload. Clem found himself falling backward to the ground by some strange, hell-bent power, and when he landed he was winded. The duke gave him no time to regain his breath, for he was a large man. He took him up by the collar and landed him a nicely planted facer before dropping him to earth again.

Thus it was at this particular moment that the magistrate, his two men, and Felicia arrived on the scene. The duke looked up and found Felicia sliding off her saddle and rushing him. Her arms went about his neck and in a soft, almost childlike voice she cried, "Oh, sir . . ." And then she raised her clear gray eyes to his face. "You are not hurt?"

He found his arms had wound themselves around her small provocative body and somehow he knew he was pleased to have her there. He gave her a squeeze, dropped a kiss on her forehead, and answered, "Of course I am not hurt, but what the devil are you doing here, minx?"

"What do you mean?" She was all eyes.

He took up her chin and said reprimandingly, "You were not supposed to come back this far." Then, dismissing the matter, he attended to more pressing ones and turned to the magistrate.

"There is another much like this—" his head indicated the man breathing hard on the ground—"all trussed up for you in the woods. However, there should be two more men returning any moment—unless, of course, they have seen what we were about and have taken to the wind. I am going to take Miss Felicia indoors and attend to the child." So saying, and with his usual air of authority, he took up Felicia's arm and led her to the cottage.

On a trestle bed in the corner of the cottage nearest the small stone fireplace was a dark wool blanket, and Felicia could see that it covered someone. She went to it and pulled it back to reveal a young woman gagged and bound at her wrists and ankles.

"Oh, faith . . . you poor thing!" Felicia cried, her hands going to her cheeks and then quickly to the cloth that had been stuffed into the young woman's small mouth. The girl was about her own age, with very fine hazel eyes and a froth of tawny curls framing her heart-shaped face.

She took a long gulp of air and gazed at Felicia before saying softly, "Thank God." It was all she said for the moment; it was all she could say.

Felicia turned to find Ashton at her side and saw that he already had a knife and was cutting through the torturing bindings that held the girl's wrists and ankles.

"What is your name? Why did those men do this to you?" Felicia inquired as she took up the girls hands and inspected her injuries, adding before she received an answer, "You will need some balm for these rope burns. Can you walk, do you think? You may ride double with me and we will take you back to the inn with us."

The girl's hazel eyes glinted appreciatively for the flash of a moment, but her head ached so from the bump she had received, and as she sat up she groaned and her hand went to her head.

"Oh . . . you poor dear . . . !" Felicia cried as she inspected the girl's head and found a rather large lump.

"Sir?" Felicia found herself unable to call him Mr. Ashton, which sounded too formal, and yet unable to call him by his given name, which would have been too forward.

It irritated him. He wasn't quite sure why. Did she think him too old? He would have her think otherwise. He said in soft tones, "Yes, love?"

"Do you think she will be able to make the trip to the inn? Perhaps there is another way of doing this?"

He frowned over the problem and said in a grave voice, "I am afraid it is the easiest and quickest way to get her to some comfort. We would otherwise have to make her wait until a coach could be fetched, and then she would nave a distance to the road, for there is no way we can get a vehicle through those woods."

Rebecca Wilson's hazel eyes flashed. "I can ride . . . really. Just don't point me at any fences today."

This made Felicia laugh and say, "That's the spirit." Then she turned and touched the duke's arm. "I know. I will leave my saddle here. It will be much more comfortable to ride double without it."

"I don't know . . ." returned the duke doubtfully.

"It is all right. I can return for it later," answered Felicia offhandedly.

"That is precisely why I am not certain it is a good idea." He then made up his mind. "Very well. I will ride with you later today and bear you company. I don't want you coming here alone."

It was on the tip of her tongue to advise him that she was quite capable of taking care of herself when she changed her mind and said in tones uncharacteristically meek for her, "That is very sweet of you, sir."

He pulled a face and started for the door, when it opened and the magistrate appeared in something of a fluster. "Mr. Ashton!"

The duke turned a frown to the older man. "Yes?"

"The other two . . . my men chased them into the woods but they got away."

"Damnation, sir! How the devil did you let them . . ." started the duke, much disturbed over this.

"They saw us . . . and before we realized, they had already turned tail and loped off. We didn't even have our horses when it happened."

The duke shook his head in disgust, thinking that he should have remained with these fools to supervise. However, there was nothing for it. "Right, then. You had better start walking the two we *do* have before they start getting resty! Do you mean to walk them all the way to town, or shall I send a conveyance to meet you?"

"What? Oh, the walk will do them good," the magistrate said with a chuckle. "Don't you worry about it, we will keep them between us."

He looked past the duke and nearly choked with surprise. "Zounds! Miss Rebecca! Never say 'twas *you* those brutes abducted? My word! Your poor father must be beside himself!"

Rebecca Wilson smiled faintly. "Indeed . . . but perhaps the sooner we leave, the sooner I may get word to him," she suggested gently.

"Indeed, indeed . . ." The magistrate looked toward Felicia and the duke. The duke had introduced himself only as Mr. Glen Ashton. He naturally assumed that Felicia was either a sister or some sort of intimate relative, for she appeared to be traveling in Mr. Ashton's company. Now he wondered about it, for Rebecca's father was a stickler for the proprieties. "Will you two be taking Miss Rebecca home? It is some distance," he asked as carefully as he could.

"We will take Miss Wilson to the inn where we are staying. There she might refresh herself before word is sent to her parent to send a coach for her journey to her home," answered Mr. Ashton with the authority that was natural to him.

The duke's cool air of command soothed the magistrate's doubts and he replied with relief, "Good. Good. I will rely on you in that matter, then."

Felicia had a sudden urge to giggle. She met Ashton's green eyes and his raised brow and controlled herself, though she could see his eyes twinkle. "I will go unsaddle my horse and bring yours along," she called as she rushed out of the cottage. This was all so exciting. She couldn't wait to get back to the inn and tell Scott.

# Chapter Ten

The duke lay back a few strides and silently observed as Felicia and Rebecca struck up a conversation on the return trip to the inn. The two girls discovered a common ground: horses, riding, jumping, and foxhounds. They discovered like spirits in each other, and a certain rapport developed. They talked, they giggled, they argued, and they agreed. Thus, the inn was reached and Miss Wilson exclaimed, "My goodness . . . here already?" Her hand went to her head and she remembered her bruises as she dismounted and gave Felicia a rueful smile. "You have almost made me forget my broken body."

"Tosh," returned Felicia offhandedly. "You are made of sturdy material. I don't doubt you are bamming us about your bruises just to get attention." This last was said with a chuckle and drew a laugh from her new friend.

Miss Wilson turned then to the duke and offered her hand. "How does one say thank you . . . for one's life?"

He bent lightly over her ungloved fingers and

smiled. "Nonsense. Your life was never in jeopardy. Only your comfort."

They all laughed at this, and Felicia took up Miss Wilson's hand and tugged her along, announcing that she would take her to her own room and see to her if "sir" would be so kind as to order tea.

"And . . . and *food*!" requested Miss Wilson over her shoulder.

It was some twenty minutes later that found Felicia, herself newly washed and changed into the only other gown she had with her, a pretty morning gown of bright yellow muslin. Her black silky hair she had brushed into gleaming waves around her pretty face, containing its luxuriant wildness with a yellow ribbon. She was bright-eyed and rosy-cheeked when she peeped in at Scott's door and found him in company with the duke.

"Oh?" she said doubtfully, the smile diminishing into uncertainty. "I . . . didn't know you two were occupied. Do I intrude?"

"Doltish female, ain't she?" said Scott, who was sitting up and grinning and seemed to be in spirits. "Get in here, do, and tell me your version of this morning's work!"

This was precisely what Felicia had wanted to do, but a form of shyness halted her. "Nonsense. I am certain Mr. Ashton gave you a good enough of account."

"Glen?" Apparently, Scott and the Duke were on first-name basis. "Well, of course he did, but what I want to know is how *you* think this morning came about." Scott was teasing and his eyes were alive with his excellent spirits.

Felicia smiled, pleased to see him looking so well.

"As usual, 'twas my nose for mischief." With this she giggled and plopped onto the bed. "Oh, Scott . . . it was just by the veriest chance. I heard these voices . . . and somehow, well, they just sounded suspicious . . . so . . ."

"So you eavesdropped. You do it so well," Scott stuck in with a gleam.

Flip put up her chin. "If you mean to be disagreeable, brat, I shan't continue."

"No, no." The duke laughed. "Do go on. I shall make certain he contains himself."

Slightly mollified, she sniffed and proceeded. "So . . . I heard them and I saw them with this bundle . . . and Scott, the bundle groaned." She waited for him to open his eyes wide and quickly went on. "Right. Wouldn't you have followed them after that?"

"Well . . ." Scott meant to think this over before giving her an answer. Answering Flip in the affirmative usually ended in trouble.

"Never mind. The groan sounded like a woman's, as I told you this morning. So I followed them . . . and then, there was Mr. Ashton, who had apparently followed me." She frowned over this and said, "Which is something I was wondering about . . ."

"Where is Miss Wilson now?" returned the duke, who had no intention of satisfying her curiosity.

"Oh, she is just resting a bit. She will come down to tea when it is ready." Felicia tilted her head, much like a pretty little bird, "Her father . . . ? Have you sent him word?"

"Yes. A groom went to Wilson Grange some minutes ago," he answered softly, for he was watching Felicia's flitting expressions.

She was satisfied with this and turned again to Scott. "Wait till you meet Becky. Oh, Scott. She is the best of all girls and she hunts with the Quorn! With the Quorn! Can you imagine? Her father takes her up there for the season."

"Never say so!" returned Scott in some astonishment, for this had indeed impressed him.

"Becky, is it?" The Duke chuckled. "It would appear you two have hit it off. You still have not used my given name, and *I* have known you longer." His green eyes caressed her, invited her to return his smile.

She did and with a blush replied, "That is different. She is a girl, you see."

"And hunts the Quorn. Would it encourage you to use my given name if I told you that I have often hunted the Quorn?"

Felicia felt her cheeks grow even hotter. "Oh, no . . . that has naught to do with it."

"What, then? Don't you consider me a friend after all we have been through together?" There was a tease in his voice, but she recognized the serious overtones as well. He had succeeded in flustering her and saw this.

"Yes, of course you are a friend," she replied hurriedly.

"Then, my name is Glen," he said softly, and he meant her to use it right then and there.

She obeyed, for his will at that moment was more hers than her own. "Glen," she said quietly and then looked up and across, her gray eyes glinting brightly as she looked into his hypnotic green eyes.

There was not time for more on this subject, for a knock sounded at the open door, and they turned to

72

find a tall, trim, pretty young woman with a mass of tawny curls in perfect disorder around her piquant face. Her gown of blue had all the indication of her ill treatment, but her carriage was such that one scarcely noticed. "Hallo," Rebecca said with a soft smile. "I hope I am not intruding?"

Felicia had been sitting on Scott's bed. She got up and went to the door, laughing as she did so. "No, how could you be, when I told you to come here to fetch us as soon as you were ready?" She turned to Scott and said proudly, "Scott Hanover, this is Miss Rebecca Wilson."

It was then that Felicia received something of a surprise, for she watched her lifelong friend gulp, blush scarlet, stammer some inconsequential amenity, and pull his quilt to his chin. She had never seen him behave just so ever before, and it was on the tip of her tongue to laughingly tease him when the duke touched her elbow and said gently, "I think refreshments are in order. I asked them to serve us in the private parlor. Scott won't mind and it will be more comfortable for Miss Wilson, I think."

She turned to the duke. He had this power over her. She couldn't name it, but she knew that it was very hard to refuse him anything. She would have preferred to sit on Scott's bed and have a jolly and totally informal tea. However, Rebecca and Scott were still strangers, she conceded to herself. Perhaps Glen . . . yes, Glen was his name. Perhaps he was right. She turned to Scott and said, "We won't be long. We are just going down to have tea."

The duke led the two ladies out of the room and then turned back to wink at Scott. "I have no doubt your irrepressible Flip will be back in no time with

Miss Wilson in tow. If you like I can have one of my shirts brought to you."

"Damn, but you are a good fellow," returned Scott gratefully.

"So I am," said the Duke with a laugh and then quickly hurried to catch up with the ladies, who were already skipping down the stairs.

Scott put back his fair head and contemplated the young woman he had just had the good fortune of meeting. Such fine bright eyes . . . and after the ordeal she had just suffered, too! Why, he rather thought she was the loveliest creature on earth. This notion elicited a long sigh before he closed his eyes and retreated into fantasy.

In the meantime, there was much excitement and havoc back at Easton Manor. Lady Daphne arrived to the intelligence that Felicia Easton and young Scott, the squire's son, had run off together, God knew where!

Lady Daphne put her gloved hand to her heart, and had her Freddy been on hand to catch her, she would have fainted right there and then and been well out of it. Freddy, however, was not on hand. Her brother, too, seemed nowhere to be found. Thus, it was that all was shoved directly into her hands as servants shrank into the background.

The squire, John Hanover, was a large man with a thatch of gray hair. He was round-bellied, he was sporting, he was fair-minded, and he was quick to temper. He did not believe for one moment that his son had eloped with little Felicia. He knew them both too well and so he told his wife. Scott's mother, however, continued to weep and fire his temper. That these children should have put him to so much trouble was beyond anything comprehensible. He didn't have the time, and so he told the lady Daphne upon entering Easton Manor.

"This—" he waved the open letter at the plump woman before him and thought that if she weren't so poor-spirited she would be a handsome woman indeed—"is all the information I have."

Lady Daphne kept cool. She had been bred to it. That was what she would have to do for now. And later? Later she would rip her brother apart with her own hands!

"Pray, sir, do be seated and calm yourself so that I may better understand the situation at hand."

"Understand? What is there not to understand? 'Tis all the fault of your dratted brother!" he retorted, his face very red.

At the moment, her opinion of her brother was much the same as the squire's. However, this was something she gave herself the right to say about the duke. She was not about to allocate the same rights to another, especially this large blustering fellow. "Squire, please, be seated and address me in a rational manner or I shall have to ask you to leave." Her tone, her face, and her demeanor were such that the squire stopped in his tracks. He considered her and decided she was indeed a handsome woman.

"Right you are, then, m'lady." He pulled up a straight-backed chair and addressed her in softer tones. "I will read you my boy's letter, though in truth I can't feel these are his words." He stretched out his arm to better view the letter in hand and read:

*"Dearest father,*

*Don't fly into the boughs and tell Mama not to be cross about all this. It is for the best. Taking Felicia away with me was the only answer to our problem. The duke was on his way, you see, so there was nothing for it but to save her and I was the only one that could do that. Can't tell you more lest you feel the need to do your duty and come after us. Mustn't do that, you know. Will see you soon, so please don't fret.*

*Scott"*

The squire looked up at the Lady Daphne and said, "Now, did you ever hear such nonsense? How could I stop his mama from being cross . . . from taking it out on me for that matter?"

"Save her from the duke?" asked Lady Daphne in a vague voice. "I don't understand. Why should she be afraid of my brother? She doesn't even know him. Rescue her from my brother? From Glen? This is absurd."

"Is it, now? Well, I will tell you what, then. Your brother wrote the poor child that he had found out she was living on her own and that he was coming here to fetch her and send her off somewhere as punishment. Got that out of Scott some days ago when he was looking all gloomy-blue." The squire shook his head. "Daft thing to do, tell her he meant to cart her off to some outlandish place. Look what has come of it."

Lady Daphne shook her head. "I see what it is. My late uncle . . . he had written to the child before he passed away, two months ago." She clucked her tongue. "I see now." She sighed. "So, your boy and Miss Easton are sweethearts? Didn't want to be separated. All very understandable."

"Gammon! Rubbish! Sweethearts indeed." He shook his head. "Haven't I made it clear they no more ran off to get married than they would set their hounds onto deer?"

She put her hand to her head. "Oh, dear . . . what are you telling me then?"

"Look, those two have been weaned together. Grew up in each other's pockets. They are more brother and sister than some are by blood. They haven't eloped. I'd lay my life on it."

"Then . . . what have they done?" She was nearly shrieking now.

"Zounds if I know, woman." He took to pacing.

"Faith!" was her response.

"Right. The question is . . . what to do? Where to go? Don't want a scandal over this, for then there would be nothing for it but to get the two married, like it or no."

She thought this over before answering. "No scandal will ensue. I shall see to that." This was something she could handle.

"No? How is that, m'lady?" he asked doubtfully.

"It will take some work, but it can be done," she answered thoughtfully as she formulated a plan in her mind.

"I will set it about that Miss Easton is abovestairs for the time being with a wretched cold. You and your lady will make sure your friends believe that your son has gone to London for you on business. It is all very simple."

"And the servants?"

"It would appear the servants here are loyal to their mistress. They kept her secret all this time regarding the absence of a chaperone on the premises . . . even from your household."

"Yes, yes . . . that may work," he answered, his mind busy with the notion. "Aye. You are more than a piece of society froth, then!" he declared as he smiled broadly and moved toward the door. "Nothing for it. I'll go and see what I can do with my wife."

"Yes indeed. She sounds a formidable lady," returned Lady Daphne.

"Aye, that ain't the half of it," he returned on a laugh.

Lady Daphne saw him to the door, where he stopped and turned to her once more. "But . . . the duke? When will he get here?"

"Soon," answered the duke's sister vaguely. Silently, she prayed, Soon, please, very soon.

# Chapter Eleven

The duke had ordered a luncheon to be served and was content to find that the innkeeper's wife had set out a simple but quite delectable selection of entrées and side dishes on the long dark oak sideboard. Hence, it was some twenty minutes before any real conversation took place, as both ladies and their gentleman companion were famished.

Flip sat back in her wooden chair with a contented sigh and commented, "Hmmm. That was good."

"Lord, Felicia," returned Rebecca on a laugh, "you shoveled that down in a thrice."

"Dreadful cat," retorted Felicia with a snort. "You haven't done so badly yourself."

"Ah, but I am entitled. I was the victim of this adventure," drawled Miss Wilson with a superior smile.

"And what is in that? All you had to do was lie there semi-conscious while *we* did all the work to rescue you!" teased Felicia. She was getting up to stretch her legs and looking toward the duke, who had excused himself a moment earlier and was standing by the window writing desk. She could see that he was composing some sort of letter, and she was curious—another of her forceful traits.

"Writing . . . Becky's father?" she asked tentatively.

He eyed her seriously, though there was a twinkle in his green eyes. "You know that I have already written to him and that we may soon find him here, in fact."

"Oh," said Felicia, wondering how to find out what he was writing and to whom.

"Hmmm. Miss Wilson's father will, I am afraid, be taking her from us any moment now," he repeated, for he was amused by her open curiosity and meant to tease her.

Felicia pulled a pout. "Drat that. It is the worst part of this whole thing."

"Oh, I don't know about that," stuck in Rebecca dryly. "I can think of a few things that were worse."

"Yes, but now that we have met . . . I shall miss you," returned Felicia with a warm smile. She had always been quick to display her emotions.

"Madcap!" Rebecca laughed. "I don't mean to stay away."

Felicia went to put her arm about her shoulders. "I don't know how it is, but I feel as though we have been friends forever, or at least . . . we will be." She then turned back toward the duke, idly asking, "Then if you are not writing to Becky's father . . . are you writing home? No doubt your wife probably wonders what has delayed you."

He refrained from grinning. "I am not married," he allowed her to know. His green eyes found hers for a long moment before he returned to the letter.

This piece of news elated her and her pleasure

gleamed on her pert face, but she pursued, for it still was not enough information. "Not married. Ah, then to your sweetheart?"

"No," he replied, and then wickedly, "I have too many of them to write them all." He did not usually allow anyone, especially a female, to pry into his business. However, he saw the smile leave her eyes and he hurried on. "I am writing my sister. I was supposed to meet her, you see, and must let her know that I am delayed on the road . . . indefinitely at the moment. We have some business we may have to postpone, as she will no doubt have to return to London and her husband."

"Oh, how mysterious that sounds!" She was fiercely curious. However, it was the moment to give him his privacy now, so she turned to Rebecca and suggested, "Come on. Let us go up and pester Scott for a bit before your father arrives."

"Perhaps we shouldn't . . . now . . . that is . . ." said Rebecca, suddenly almost shy.

"Why not?" Felicia was surprised.

"He may be tired . . . not up to it . . . and I should go home and change my gown. It is so very soiled."

"Nonsense. Scott doesn't care for such things, and he has rested alone all this time." Flip was already leading the way out of their private dining parlor, saying over her shoulder, "He is probably bored to tears up there alone."

Rebecca got to her feet and looked toward the duke, who offered gently, "I think it would be good for the boy to have your company. He will be more comfortable now. I provided him with a shirt so that he wouldn't have to greet you in his nightclothes."

Rebecca smiled at him and then heard Flip impatiently calling her name, so she answered, "I am coming!"

The duke looked after them and smiled. His little Felicia was certainly something of a whirlwind force, hard to deny and so very attractive. . . .

The afternoon had progressed. Miss Wilson's father had arrived and whisked his daughter off, with heartfelt thanks to everyone. There was one awkward moment when the duke met the older gentleman's eye and found himself feeling a twinge of guilt as he continued the lie. He introduced himself not as the Duke of Somerset, but as Glen Ashton. However, he told himself that it didn't matter, as he probably would never see either Rebecca or her father again. He then turned to the problem of Felicia's saddle.

"Hadn't we better be thinking of riding to the cottage and fetching your saddle?" He discovered that he was rather looking forward to the ride with Felicia.

She had been in the midst of teasing Scott about Rebecca, for she had noticed his disappointment at her departure. Thus, on a laugh she turned her face to the duke and her eyes twinkled enough to mesmerize him as she answered, "Oh, yes, we should, for I daresay it will start to get dark before we get back if we don't leave now." She found his hand on hers and a sure thrill tingled her spine as he led her out of Scott's room. She turned to Scott and with a naughty laugh bantered, "My . . . you don't look half so blue to lose me."

"Blue be hanged!" answered her lifelong friend. "I'm that pleased to be rid of you for an hour or two." He mitigated this with an affectionate smile and added, "Flip, be a love and see if they won't serve us all dinner up here in my room. I do so hate eating alone."

Both Felicia and the duke answered that they would arrange this with pleasure, and then they were off. While a groom saddled one of the duke's fine dark bay carriage horses, Glen Ashton took Felicia's chestnut gelding and led him outdoors, where he slipped the horse's bridle on and called her to order.

"Come on, girl." He frowned, for she was busy inspecting a newcomer's horse in the mud paddock. "Felicia!"

She turned and, wide-eyed, apologized at once. "Sorry, but *he* is handsome."

The duke glanced at the snowy gray gelding grazing on a flake of hay in the small turn-out and mumbled something about the horse being well enough. "Now, come on, and I will give you a leg up."

She eyed him. He seemed cross. Why? Because she had been looking at the snowy gray? She noticed that the owner of this animal was still standing nearby and that he was smiling at her. She turned to look at Ashton in time to see him level a withering look at the young man. Suddenly she wanted to giggle, but she controlled herself. He hoisted her up on the count of three, and she adjusted her skirts around herself as he went to fetch his own horse. During this time the young man standing at the turn-out sidled over to Felicia's horse and, without meeting her eye, petted her horse's neck and said lightly, "No saddle? May I offer my own?"

"You may not!" It was almost the sound of thunder and it came from the duke.

The young man was summarily dealt with, and

stammering something incoherent, he mumbled himself backward until he was out of their view and on his way into the inn. He had only meant to stop for an hour or so and grab a bite to eat before continuing his journey. He thought now that it would be best if he proceeded with that intention, as the tall well-dressed man looked like trouble.

The duke put his hand on Felicia's bent knee and felt her tremble beneath the cloth of her gown, and for no reason at all it thrilled him. Her eyes were glistening with amusement, and she spoke before he had the opportunity. "You were quite dreadful to that poor young man. He was only being polite."

"He was ogling you and deserved worse than he got."

She laughed. "Nonsense. Come on, then, my sir, for I daresay it will soon be getting dark."

"As you command, m' lady," he said grandly, giving her a mock bow.

Again she laughed and this time urged her horse forward. He called after her to be careful and remember that she was without a saddle.

"I have been riding for as long as I can remember and often without a saddle. It is safe enough . . . though *not* comfortable."

He jogged until he was beside her. His bay nipped at Flip's horse and he reprimanded him. During this moment, she watched him and found herself tingling from her toes to her eyebrows. He was so very handsome with his uncovered head of ginger-brown hair blowing freely in the wind. His shoulders were broad, his waist narrow, and his legs long and muscular. Such a man! Then there was the twinkle that would light up his emerald eyes, the smile that would seduce her out of the worst of moods. Stop! She would have to stop thinking of him in these terms.

"And so you have run wild"— he chuckled—"but if you mean to make your entrance into the Polite World of London, you will have to adopt the manners of a lady."

She turned her face to his, suddenly grave. "Am I behaving like anything else?"

He had the sudden urge to grab hold of her, to tell her that she was the most refreshing lady of his acquaintance, to tell her . . . absurd! This was absurd. He had only just met her and she was a veritable schoolgirl, with hoydenish manners. He answered diplomatically, "You are very much the lady, my dear, because *I* can see through your earthy veneer. Not all our members of society bother to look that closely."

"*I* may not care for the opinions of those who do not bother to look past one's veneer," she answered, her chin well up and looking very much a duchess.

"Bravo!" He smiled fondly at her. "Now, *that* is how a lady behaves."

They bantered on in this style, about manners, hers and society's. She ventured questions about some of the famous fashionables and listened raptly to his descriptions, until all at once she noticed they had reached the cottage in the woods.

"Oh my!" she exclaimed in some surprise. "We are here already." She moved to slide off her horse and when she turned found him there, for he had meant to assist her.

"And that is another thing you will have to learn," he said softly.

"What is?" She couldn't breathe with him so very

close. Such green eyes he had! How brightly they gleamed!

"To allow a gentleman to assist you, even if you *can* do it yourself."

"Always? Must I always allow every gentleman that comes along to assist me?" She was being coy. She knew that she was but couldn't help herself.

"No," he said firmly and had his arms around her as his mouth closed on hers. Her lips were sweet and her body tempting him to crush her in his hold. His kiss lingered into another and then he was parting her lips, gently probing with his tongue, teaching her to respond.

When he let her up for air, she managed a smile and said softly, "Is that another thing I must learn?"

"No again, love. You need no lesson there." He then put her aside with some resolution and moved toward the cottage, saying only, "Stay with the horses."

She did, but her eyes followed him in total adoration. Here now was a man! Here was more than just a man, but *the* man of her dreams.

# Chapter Twelve

It was a bright morning, but that was the only good thing about it, thought the lady Daphne as she surveyed her breakfast with some disgust. She had already sustained yet another visit from the squire about the runaways and it was still not yet ten o'clock!

He had ranted and raved, for his wife had cried most of the night, or so the squire had reported. The problem, he told her roundly, was now hers. Well, if that didn't go beyond anything! Freddy! Perhaps it was time to send for her dear Freddy? He would know what to do. He always knew what to do. No! He would tell her to wash her hands of the entire mess and come home.

What, then? After all, Freddy would be right if he said such a thing. It wasn't her problem but her wayward brother's. Drat the man! Where was he? God only knew. It was at this juncture in her thoughts that the Easton butler arrived at her table with a note neatly displayed on a silver salver. He bent in fine form and offered this to her with an apology. "My lady. I am so very sorry, but it appears this letter arrived for you yesterday."

She took up the sealed envelope at once, for she knew her brother's handwriting, and said, "Yesterday? Why wasn't it brought to me at once?"

He pulled a face. " 'Twas the new day girl. I was in the back helping Cook with some of the heavy chores, so the new girl got the door. Some lad brought it for you. She went to give it to you, but you were out taking a stroll, my lady." He sighed and then continued, "She being new and all, well, she put it down on the wall table in the hall, thinking to tell me about it, and went about her chores, you see. . . ."

"She forgot to tell you." Lady Daphne dismissed him with a raised brow. "Very well, but do speak to her about this."

"Indeed, m'lady, I already have."

Daphne was impatient to read, so she tore open the envelope and found:

*Dearest Daffy, best of all females,*

*I am delayed. Perhaps you should return to London, for I have a notion that if I keep you kicking your heels at Easton for too much longer both you and your Freddy will have my head!*

*Forgive me. Tell the child I shall try and fetch her before the end of the month and mean to make it up to her.*

*Yours,*
*Glen*

"Well!" said the lady Daphne out loud and understandably enraged. "This is too much! Best of all females, is it? Ha!" This is intolerable. How dare he put the poor Easton girl off like that? What if she had been here, desperately waiting for him to fetch her to London for her season, poor thing? It is no wonder she ran away.

This was Lady Daphne's reasoning, and then she remembered that the child had run away from him rather than allow him to descend on her. Well, she was not going to hobble back to London and leave things in such a mess. How could she? And she wasn't going to stay at Easton with the squire bowling down on her every other moment. There were two runaways afoot, one of whom her brother was responsible for!

She was going to find her wayward brother and drag him by the ears into displaying a sense of his duty toward this poor girl of his! If it was the last thing she did on this earth, it was going to be done. She would find him and she would hand this mess into his keeping. In this mood, she rose from her breakfast table to hunt out the butler and find out where the letter had come from. Ha! Did Glen think she couldn't track him if she wanted to do so? Ha!

He was almost nine years her senior! More than that, he was an experienced man about town, a rakehell, while she . . . ? She was an innocent. He had no right to toy with her in this outrageous fashion. Such were the duke's thoughts as he moved into the cottage and took up her saddle and girth. Just what are you doing, Glen Ashton, Duke of Somerset?

Yet, her gray eyes won a response from him he could not name. Her rough-and-tumble manners tickled him, and her lush beauty filled him with desire. He couldn't remember ever having felt quite like this before. He moved outdoors once more and went to her chestnut. The saddle pad was already in place, as Felicia had used it on her way there, so he had only to drop the saddle lightly onto the horse's back and tighten the girth. Felicia watched him in quiet.

He regretted kissing her. She sensed it, knew it, was hurt by it. Well, she was a reasonable girl, so she thought it out. Of course, he regretted it. He was a man of honor. He has no intention of doing the honorable and is probably berating himself for dallying with an innocent girl. There was that. What to do? Must make him remember her, even if it meant being outrageous. She waited for him to turn and smile.

"Come on, Felicia, up you go."

"Right now?" she asked and moved in place. She was molding herself against his body, tilting her face provocatively, inviting him with her eyes.

"Right now!" he said firmly, almost gravely.

She pouted. "Oh, sir?" She bolstered her courage and dove right in. "Do you only dole out one kiss a day? Must I wait till tomorrow for another?"

He was surprised into laughing heartily and flicking her nose. "Temptress, you are lucky enough to be playing with a fire that doesn't wish to burn you."

"I don't mind a little singeing. . . ." She had her hands around his neck and got on tiptoes to place a kiss upon his lips.

He was startled by the passion she aroused in him, and he pulled out of her embrace. "Flip!" And then quickly, "Come on, it is already dark and Scott will be worried."

She laughed. "You are afraid of me."

"Afraid of you?" he was just a bit irritated, for this hit home.

"Hmmm. You certainly can't ruin my honor by giving me a little kiss out here in the woods, so you must be afraid it might lead to more, and here I thought you a gallant, always in control."

"I am always in control, which means I do the kissing when I wish to," he said gravely.

This deflated her, and her smile disappeared instantly.

"Oh" was all she could think to say.

He laughed and this time dropped a kiss upon the top of her head before giving her a leg up. "That's a good girl," he said jovially and took up his own horse.

Good girl, indeed! What a dreadful notion, to be thought of as a dull, good ol' girl! Well, he had kissed her and written her off as unexciting. How very lowering such a thought was. The trip home was *not* spent in lively conversation. In fact, the duke found his questions answered in monosyllables and grunts, so he soon gave up the effort and fell into deep thought himself.

Dinner was served, as Scott had requested, within the cozy confines of his bedroom. A fire was lit, he was in good spirits, and still the air seemed filled with tension. He wasn't considered a particularly perceptive young man, but he couldn't mistake the unhappiness in Felicia's gray eyes, or the grim set of Glen Ashton's thin lips. When he had done with his dessert, he pushed the tray away and watched Flip as she moved to take it from him and put it outside the door for the servant. He eyed her and made yet another attempt to break the ice.

"Well, well . . . what say you, Flip, to a game of cards?"

"Not I. Perhaps you and . . . Mr. Ashton," she answered softly.

"Come now," said Mr. Ashton, his tone rather touched with annoyance. "Surely you cannot deny us a little game of cards?"

She eyed him and realized that she was pouting still. How dreadful she must appear! She attempted a smile and said, "Oh, if that is what you really want." Then, more like herself, "I will go and fetch the cards, though I won't play cribbage!"

She was sent to look for a deck of playing cards in the private morning parlor and was busy at this task when she felt a shiver run up her spine. She spun around with a startled motion to find Ashton there, standing very near.

"Faith! You made me jump," she exclaimed and then found herself blushing.

"Did I? I certainly did not have that end in mind." His voice was low, husky. He had her shoulders, and her name was on his lips, though it was scarcely audible. "Ah, Felicia . . ." And then he was kissing her. He hadn't meant to do this. He had an affection for the girl, and he didn't want to do this! Yet watching her all through dinner, seeing her dejection, knowing he was the cause, had made him feel an even greater cad than he had felt when he kissed her earlier that day. This was all wrong! He had to stop. He pushed her away from him just as he discovered he was parting her lips, tasting her tongue with his own, and he felt himself in agony.

"You are driving me mad!" he said on the note of a growl.

"As you are me," she answered softly.

"Find the cards" was all he could say as he turned abruptly from her and left the room. This was too much, too soon. It was dangerous. He didn't know what he felt, but he knew he didn't want to feel this way.

Felicia watched him leave and her heart skipped. Mercy, she exclaimed to herself, she was in love! Totally, completely, devastatingly in love. He was virtually a stranger, and yet everything about him touched a chord, a need within herself. Well, well, Miss Easton, here is a challenge indeed. A man among men. A London beau, a Corinthian who has probably had dozens of interesting and beautiful women. You don't stand a chance. Her heart answered her mind: Have to . . . must have a chance!

# Chapter Thirteen

Scott felt the sun warm against his face and smiled. He was feeling good, and strong. It was well after nine o'clock. Where the deuce was Flip? She had stopped by earlier that morning, stolen a piece of his toast, sipped at his hot chocolate, and said she was going out for a morning ride. Well, she should have been back by now. He sighed. The doctor had been paying him daily visits, and although the prognosis was excellent, he had been forbidden to exercise just yet. Hence, Scott was getting restless.

Well, he would just get up and take a short walk to the hallway, where he might have a peep. He pulled off his covers and swung his legs around to the floor, and there he stopped. Dizzy. He was actually dizzy. This was ridiculous. Why should he be dizzy? Well, he just wouldn't allow his body to betray him. With some determination he got to his feet and stood. There. He was up. It occurred to him that he was also queasy. Hell, suddenly he felt just a bit off balance. Walk! That was what he needed, to walk and get his land legs back in order. He got to the door, swung it open, and felt his world start to spin, and spin, and then spin some more.

Rebecca handed her gray gelding to the stableboy and made her way into the inn and up the stairs. It never occurred to her that she would not find Felicia within; after all, the hour, even in the country, was early. She was dressed in her pale blue riding habit. It was trimmed in black at the collar with ornate black buttons down the jacket's tailored center. A black silk top hat rested on her pretty tawny curls, and its netting had been pushed away from her face and onto the hat's crown. She looked charming.

She didn't find anyone in the inn's main gallery and took to the stairs, where she was startled to find Scott tottering within his doorway. "Scott!" she exclaimed, for he looked as though he was about to faint.

He saw an angel in blue and smiled. "Miss Wilson . . ." It was scarcely an audible sound.

She was quick-witted and nimble. She screamed for the innkeeper and dove to save Scott from falling to the floor. She caught him by the waist and took the brunt of his weight onto her side and then looked for somewhere nearby to deposit him.

It was at this moment that Felicia and the duke walked in, both laughing over some jest. They stopped short. Felicia's hand went to her mouth, and the duke took to the stairs, putting them away two by two. "Here!" he commanded, taking Rebecca's burden from her.

The duke carried Scott, cradlelike, to the boy's bed and there deposited him as gently as he was able.

Scott opened his eyes, blushed, and stammered an apology. "Sorry . . ."

"Preposterous boy." The duke smiled compassionately at him. "You have lost too much blood to be up and about just yet. Give it a little more time, and I tell you what. I shall give you a series of leg exercises you may do while you sit in your bed. How is that?"

"Famous," said Scott, pulling himself up into a sitting position and glancing toward the girls.

"Hallo," said Rebecca as his eyes rested on her. "I think I know how you feel. Being confined is a most intolerable sensation, but I brought you the morning paper. . . ." She went forward with it, and as he took it from her their eyes met once more.

He thanked her with some profuseness, and it was Felicia who giggled over this circumstance, exclaiming that it was only a newspaper, after all!

So stating, she went and plopped a kiss upon his head and announced her intention of getting breakfast, ". . . for I am half-starved to death." She looked at Rebecca. "Have you eaten, Becky?"

"Yes, but I will join you anyway and have another cup of coffee."

"Yes, but . . . you can't leave me," whined Scott, putting his hand to his heart. "You were kind enough to bring me the morning paper and now leave me to it on my own?"

"Well, whatever can you mean?" Rebecca was surprised into asking.

"I am too weak to be left on my own. I need you to read the paper to me . . . from cover to cover." Scott was grinning.

Becky laughed. "Very well." She turned to Felicia. "You two go on. I will join you presently."

Felicia giggled and moved out of the room, stayed a moment, and called over her shoulder with an admonishing finger, "Scott Hanover, you are the most complete hand!"

The duke winked at him before he followed Felicia out of the room and added to this, "Indeed, and a lad after my own heart."

At Easton Manor, Lady Daphne went about the business of discovering how the note from her brother had been delivered. After that fact was established, it was an easy enough task to find out that the groom who had delivered it had come from the Andover Inn, off the Post Road to London. This establishment, she was advised, was a perfectly respectable hostelry some twelve miles west and should not take her above two hours' traveling time.

It took her, however, some length of time to see that her maid packed her bags, to instruct the household to carry on, and to compose a letter of sorts to the good squire, whom she was very certain would visit the Easton establishment before the day was out. With this worry in mind, she rushed her coachman to hitch up the horses and proceed with the journey.

With something of a contented sigh she relaxed against the squabs of her comfortable conveyance and eyed her maid, who was chattering about nonsense in the most pleasing of fashions, for she could listen without offering comment. In this manner she passed the first twenty minutes of her trip. However, with something close to vexation she nearly stomped her foot as she felt the carriage come to a stop.

"What is it?" she called out her window. "Why are we stopping?"

"Sorry, m'loidy," offered her coachman. "Brownie 'ere lost a shoe. But don't ye be fretting it, oi 'ad the good sense to 'ave 'ere extras, oi do!"

"Good man," returned Lady Daphne, and as she sat back this time it was to gleefully plan her brother's murder!

Breakfast had been a meal Felicia thought she would never forget. This was not due to the innkeeper's homemaid biscuits and buns. It wasn't due to the innkeeper's fresh eggs and tasty sausages. In fact, what made it so had little to do with what she ate, as she found she couldn't eat. Felicia had fallen in love.

She stared at him in wide-eyed wonder as he spoke and recounted amusing anecdotes about his youth, his schooldays, his hunting experiences. She choked with laughter as he elaborated on these incidents. She blushed with confusion when he reached out and fondly caressed her cheek, and she very nearly threw her arms around him when he bent to drop a kiss lightly on her nose.

What was she going to do? She adored him. He was wonderful. He was beautiful. His eyes were delicious in their green depths. His shoulders were so broad, his air so self-assured, so confident. He was everything she had dreamed a man should be, could be, and he was above her touch. What would he want with *her*?"

Her mood went from mountain high to a plunging below sea level. She couldn't win him. He had every woman in London to choose from. He could have anyone, and here she was in an old traveling gown that had little style and less appeal. He noticed her sudden despondency and frowned.

"What is it, minx? What has you blue-deviled?"

"Oh . . . naught. I was just thinking," she answered quietly and did not look at him.

He studied her and put his arm around her comfortingly, drawing her near as he uplifted her chin with his fingers. Odd, how the nearness of her sent a sure thrill through his body. Why the deuce was he so very attracted to this one?

"Thinking about moving on to London, no doubt, before your guardian catches you. Well, don't you worry, he can't have at you with me about."

"You won't be about forever," she returned softly.

He frowned again. "Do you know, I can't imagine what that might be like. It seems I have formed an absurd attachment to you and Scott. I should like to see you safely established and don't mean to let you go until I have that accomplished."

She dimpled and got on tiptoes to kiss his cheek. He turned slightly and their lips met instead. It was like an explosion for them both. Fire! He was on fire, he thought, and drew back immediately. Faith! Oh, faith, what had she done? she asked herself and dropped her gaze to the floor.

He broke the sudden tension of the moment with a chuckle and said, "Come on, we had better go see what those two are doing upstairs." This was preposterous. Why the devil did she have such an effect on him?

They gathered a tray of snacks, proceeded up the stairs, and descended upon Scott and Becky with jesting and gaiety. Becky was biting into a piece of toast and complaining about Scott, who she said made her read until she had no voice left. This set up a round of bantering, so that no one heard the sound of carriage wheels on the cobblestone courtyard outdoors. Some moments later, a lady of much style and stature made her way up the stairs toward the sound of laughter, for she was very sure she recognized one voice amongst the group.

She viewed the scene that met her eyes with a great deal of warranted indignation, and her hands went to her hips as she exclaimed in outraged accents, "Well! And so my brother the duke, *here you are*!"

He jumped to his feet and moved across the room to her, crying out with a laugh, for she looked so very annoyed.

"Daffy! So I am, but what are *you* doing here?"

"What am I doing here? How dare you! Let me tell you that I have spent the most dreadful two days of my life on your infamous errand. Dutifully, obediently, I went to Easton to meet and care for your ward. Well, you were not the only one that was not there to meet me!" She was near to shouting and totally disregarded the fact that three pairs of strangers' eyes were wide open and studying her with great interest.

"What do you mean?" the duke inquired, his brows coming together.

"She ran away! That is what I mean. There I was being berated by the squire, who thinks she absconded with his son for God only knows where, for one moment he tells me he can't believe they would elope and then the next he tells me that is what they must have done, and where were you? Here, having a jolly old time. . . ." She broke off and noticed the other people in the room. She recalled her manners and said in their general direction, "Oh, how do you do? I know you will hate to lose his company, but I feel I must steal my brother from you for a moment or two. I do promise to give him back, perhaps not all in one piece, but return him I certainly shall, for after today I doubt that I shall ever bother with him again." She eyed her brother and said, "You will join me downstairs, Glen." So demanding, she turned on her heel and left him to make his apologies.

He did, and then rushed out of the room. Disbelief was the first sensation that Felicia was struck with as she watched him follow his sister out of the room. That woman had called him a duke. He was due to meet her at Easton. Here . . . faith have mercy, was her guardian the duke!

She looked to Scott, who had come to the same conclusion, and groaned, "Oh . . . no . . . Scott . . ." It was scarcely an audible sound.

"I can't believe it," said Scott. "*He* is not old!"

"What are you two talking about?" asked Becky, eyeing them as though they had lost their minds. "What is going on?"

"What are we going to do?" cried Felicia, ignoring Becky's wide-eyed question. "Scott . . . what are we going to do?" To herself she said, What are you going to do? You have kissed your guardian. You have fallen in love with your guardian. You have lied to him. . . .

"Come clean," said Scott bracing himself. "Naught else to do." He thought about this as she moaned and decided, "Not so bad, after all. If he is your guardian, seems to me, all has turned out for the best. You like him."

Felicia eyed her longtime friend with horror, and

101

then did something he had rarely—if ever—seen her do. She burst into tears! Becky went to her immediately and put her arm about her shoulders and attempted to soothe her.

"Flip . . . stop it . . . try and tell me what has happened. Flip?"

Scott watched, for he was momentarily at a loss and he looked to Rebecca to set things right.

Felicia groaned and flopped down on the edge of the bed and declared, "My life is ruined!"

"Is it?" returned Becky calmly and sat beside her. "How very dreadful, especially when it has hardly begun. Start at the beginning, Flip, and perhaps we might be able to muddle through this thing together."

Felicia sniffed, took up one of the clean linens on the side table beside Scott's elbow, and blew her nose, "Right. I will start at the beginning."

Belowstairs an outraged Lady Daphne paced, her arms folded across her middle, as she lectured her younger brother. In detail she described her ordeal of the last few days, turning on him now and then to wag a finger in a threatening fashion as she recalled the squire's behavior toward her. It did not occur to her until she was more than three-quarters through her diatribe that her brother was taking this badly. Usually he laughed such things off, but here he was, looking pale and stunned.

She relented a trifle and eyed him thoughtfully. "Well, after all, one cannot set all the blame at your door, Glen. It seems there is some explanation for the girl's queer behavior. Our uncle had discovered that she was living unchaperoned and wrote a severe, lecturing letter, telling her that he was on his way to take her to some outlandish place in the wilds of Cornwall. Pity, but I don't suppose he knew just how to handle a young female. He seems to have frightened the poor girl sufficiently, for when she received news of the duke's arrival in the area, she fled with her dearest friend—the squire's son. Apparently, she had no idea that our uncle had passed on. . . ." She surveyed his reaction and, puzzled, inquired, "What is it? Why do you look like that?"

"Never mind . . . go on." He was feeling very nearly sick. It had been bad enough that he had found himself flirting outrageously with a young, unprotected girl, but to discover that she was his ward, that he was her guardian, made him feel suddenly miserable.

"Go on?" she retorted impatiently. "Don't you see? She is your ward! While I can't find it in my heart to blame the girl for her flight, I can see that it will bring down a scandal about our heads if we don't find them, and quickly, before the gossipmongers get wind of this."

The Duke of Somerset ran his hands through his thick waves of ginger-colored hair and groaned. "Well, Daffy, we don't have far to look. They are, the both of them, upstairs." With this he sank back against his chair and closed his eyes.

"Glen?" cried Lady Daphne. "What are you saying?"

He opened his eyes and said quietly, "Rest easy, Daphne."

"Rest easy? Are you mad? Do you mean to tell me that your ward and the squire's son have been with you all this time? How is this?" She took up a wooden chair and sat down heavily, apparently overcome.

"Until this moment I did not realize Felicia was my ward," he answered quietly.

"Did you not? Did you not think it odd that a young woman and a young man were traveling about the countryside unattended? Did you not find it a coincidence that she carried your ward's given name?"

He looked abashed. "I hadn't realized my ward's given name was Felicia." He shook his head. "I had never given it much thought."

"You may tell me everything, Glen," commanded his sister.

He did not tell her everything, but he did give her enough information to satisfy her. When he had done so, he sighed and offered, "You may write a letter to the squire and the Grange, advising them all that my ward and young Scott have been with me all along. Tell them that Scott was injured fighting off highwaymen, if you must, but make it clear that they were never alone."

"No, no. They will wonder what Scott and Felicia were doing out at night together. I shall write the squire the truth and have him set it about that his wife and Scott had delivered Felicia to you in London . . . and that Scott stayed on there. That will have to serve."

"Servants?"

"Loyal to both families, from what I could see." She was frowning over this. She then looked directly into his eyes and said sadly, "I thought perhaps you might be starting to take your life seriously. You have responsibilities to your title, to your heritage, to your family, and to this poor ward of yours, yet here you are raking mad as ever . . . hell-bent as ever . . ."

He reached out and covered her hand with his. "Aye, and this girl of mine, she is much the same. Daff . . . you will have to help me in this."

"Help you? How can I when you will not help yourself?"

"I want to establish my ward properly. I want her the toast of London . . . I want her happy."

"Do you?"

"Indeed." He smiled. "She is a taking little thing. I believe you two will deal famously together."

She was surprised. There had been affection in his voice when he spoke of his ward. This was something new. Well, well, perhaps this new responsibility might be the making of him yet. She inclined her head. "Very well." She got to her feet and with some resolution said, "Come then, Glen, and introduce us."

He grinned wickedly. Damn, but he wanted to see his Flip's face when she discovered who he was! She had lied to him, and for that he meant her to have a punishment of sorts. What that punishment would be he had not quite decided yet, but see to it he most certainly intended to do.

Abovestairs, Becky had listened to the tale with some keen interest. When it was done she had an urge to giggle, but instead smiled softly and said, "Silly pea-goose. This is wonderful. Your guardian is a friend and he is a Corinthian . . . a nonpareil. He will be able to give you entrée into the best of London's society. You will have a wondrous season. What is there to be miserable about?"

Flip glanced toward Scott. She couldn't very well tell Becky she was in love with her guardian with Scott sitting there listening to every word. Instead, she simply said, "He lied to me. He never said he was the duke."

"He probably thought you would be more comfortable not knowing about his title. He would have told you in the end," said Becky reasonably.

"Yes but . . ." Felicia attempted to get her point across, but the doorway was shadowed as the duke and his sister arrived on the scene. Felicia eyed him poutingly, accusingly, but said nothing.

He saw the look and was amused. Certes, he thought, the chit is annoyed with me! Amazing little brat . . . brazen to the last.

# Chapter Fourteen

Lady Daphne was curious in spite of the fact that she was loath to witness the inevitable scene her brother would no doubt provoke. She settled her dilemma by taking up a corner chair and folding her hands in her lap. There, she thought, a perfect unobtrusive vantage point. She was, of course, quite incorrect.

Her brother turned to her and then to Scott and Felicia almost simultaneously and said in his easy sophisticated voice, "Allow me to introduce you to my sister." His chin moved imperceptibly toward Felicia and he continued, "Miss Felicia Easton, my ward. Mr. Scott Hanover, her friend. Miss Rebecca Wilson, yet another of Felicia's friends." He turned to his sister, who was now attempting to retain her composure. "My sister, Lady Daphne Waverly."

If he thought to discompose Felicia, he had yet something to learn. She was angry with him. Angry with this move, angry with the situation, and therefore much in command of herself. Her chin was well up as she said, "But you, sir? You have not introduced yourself, though I take it from your reference to my position as your ward, that you are my guardian, the Duke of Somerset.''

Scarcely did he blink. He inclined his head and restrained an urge to chuckle. ''Indeed, child. So it appears.''

''I think I shall go home,'' said Rebecca, getting to her feet and smiling apologetically toward Lady Daphne.

Felicia grabbed at her hand. ''No, Becky . . . please do not.''

There was such a pleading look in Flip's gray eyes that Becky felt a wave of guilt. She wanted no part in what she thought was going to be a major confrontation, yet she couldn't leave Felicia to her own devices. She couldn't leave Scott, for he looked as though he might faint. She said nothing, but sat back down near her friend.

Scott thought it time he spoke. ''I . . . I may be able to . . . explain,'' he squeaked.

The duke's mobile brow went up and his green eyes glittered. ''Perhaps it is not necessary. Perhaps I understand the confusion that has occurred.''

''Do you?'' retorted Felicia getting to her feet. There was deep color in her cheeks. ''Then *perhaps* you may explain to us!''

He did laugh then, for she looked adorable in her heat. Such a spitfire, she was. He glanced at his sister, who was now watching with some intensity. ''Indeed. The letter you originally had was written by my late uncle. I have recently inherited the title and the pleasure of your guardianship.'' His eyes were twinkling as they met her gray gold-flecked orbs, and he could see her mind working.

She got right to the point. "Now what, your Grace?"

He frowned. It disturbed him to hear her formal use of his title, but there was little he could do about that just now.

"It is my intention to do what I started out to do in Easton." He inclined his head toward his silent sister. "My sister Daphne was to meet me at Easton, where we meant to take you up between us and haul you off to London." He was absolutely grinning now. "Monsters that we are, we thought you might rather enjoy a London season."

She looked away from them both and then to Scott, before she returned her gaze to the duke. "And now?"

"And now, we will remain here until Scott is in safe hands and then we will continue our journey to London. There, you will find yourself chaperoned by an elderly but quite dear cousin of mine while you are installed in my household. My sister has been kind enough to offer to take you shopping and routing about."

"Oh" was all Felicia felt herself capable of saying, and then, "But Scott . . . Becky . . ."

"May visit you in London, and both will be invited to the ball we are planning in honor of your entrance into society."

Felicia was frightened. At home, in her own environment, she was secure unto herself. At Easton, with Scott at her side, her friends all about, she was at ease, she was poised and confident that she could take on the world. Here was something new. No, this was not an old duke, and no, he was not sending her off to nowhere, but she suddenly wanted to run away again. He was taking her to London, where she would know virtually no one. He was presenting her to a world of fashionables, where she would feel lost and out of place. Desperately she clung to her old familiar needs. "I don't want to go to London, I don't want to enter society and I don't want a ball! I want to stay at Easton and ride and hunt with Scott." It was almost a wail.

In two strides the duke was near her and his arms enfolded her. Oddly enough, she dove into his embrace, and for a moment neither said a word. She sniffled, however, as she held back her tears, and he kissed the top of her head. "Do you think, my little zany, that I will allow you to feel one moment's discomfort?" He held her shoulders. "Do you?"

She shook her head and sniffled again, for she trusted him, absurdly she trusted him. He held her again for a brief moment and then set her back. "There. Then I don't want anymore nonsense."

His sister was watching this with wide-eyed amazement. She had never seen her brother exert himself on any woman's behalf before. Here was this slip of a girl . . . and Glen . . . well, Glen was not just doing his duty. There was something else. Why, he almost seemed involved. No. Impossible. Not Glen, and not with a schoolgirl!

Felicia turned to Rebecca. "Will you come stay with us in London?"

Lady Daphne interjected kindly, "Indeed, I think that would be very pleasant."

Rebecca glanced from Lady Daphne to the duke and said softly that she rather thought her father would not mind if she spent some time in London.

"Good!" announced Scott. "Then that settles it,

for I mean to do the same." He grinned and looked at the duke. "Looks as though you have the lot of us, your Grace."

"God give me strength!" The duke laughed.

On that note Felicia dimpled at him and in a voice more her own asked, "Well, when do we leave?"

# Chapter Fifteen

Felicia sat curled up on the Somerset Town House's very luxurious yellow damask sofa. Her rich black hair had been trimmed and styled in a profusion of fashionable curls piled in adorable clusters around her piquant face. Her morning gown of amber velvet suited her provocative curves, and she presented quite a picture. Idly, she was fingering the morning paper, now and then glancing at the duke, who sat at his desk going through his morning mail.

The library doors were wide open, and through them Cousin Amelia glided, announcing that the hour was quite late and asking why Felicia was not ready.

Cousin Amelia was seventy years old, she was sweet, she was dear, she was flighty, forgetful, and at times quite amusing in her fashion. However, Felicia had been installed in London now for more than three weeks. She had been pushed, prodded, and made into a fashionable miss. She was heartily tired of it. Lady Daphne meant to take her this morning to some dressmaker's for yet another series of gowns, and Felicia did not wish to go. She wanted to spend the morning near her duke. She pouted and retorted impatiently, "I am not ready because I am not going."

"Not going? But dearest, Daphne will be here any moment."

Cousin Amelia, Lady Daphne, and most of the household staff had discovered that while Miss Felicia was one of the most soft-hearted young ladies of their acquaintance, she could also be quite headstrong once her mind was made up. Cousin Amelia glanced toward the duke. It had also been noticed that while Felicia would defy all others, she had never yet been able to refuse the duke in any of his requests.

The duke smiled but said nothing for the moment, leaving Amelia on her own.

Amelia attempted reason. "Daphne has made this appointment especially for you. You cannot imagine how many mamas are after Madame Dumont to make gowns for their daughters, yet she accepted to do so for you."

"Well, now she doesn't have to be so condescending. She can make room for another mama's daughter and Daffy will not have to be obligated to such a conceited person," came Flip's reply.

The duke laughed out loud and got up from his desk; he moved to take up his Felicia's chin, noting to himself that she was quite the most beautiful creature he had ever seen. "This sounds interesting, minx. I think I will accompany you and my sister to this conceited dressmaker this morning and see if she can do you justice."

Felicia beamed, her whole world suddenly brighter. "I shall run up and fetch my bonnet and spencer and be back in a moment."

113

Amelia watched the girl bounce out of the room and turned to her cousin. "She quite adores you."

"I am her guardian," he answered on a frown. "I should hope she would care for me."

"Indeed?" returned Amelia but dropped it at that, for she could see that it was not a subject he would discuss.

The truth was, it was a subject which he thought of all the time. Felicia. Her name was forever on his lips, curving them into a smile. She bubbled around his home. She bounced into a room like a fresh spring breeze and she brought laughter with her. She found life amusing and was forever pointing out this or that and making him chuckle over it. He looked at people through her eyes and found new dimensions. Felicia.

Ah, so what, then? What? Very easy to answer, actually. Soon, very soon, he would watch her waltz into society, catch some man's eye, and waltz out of his life. What, then, would life be like? Never mind. This was nonsense. She was an entertaining interlude, and when she was gone, something, someone would take her place. It was how he answered himself.

Amelia picked up her crochet needles and wool and made herself comfortable. It was so pleasant here at Somerset House with Glen and Felicia. She felt she belonged. They never made her feel as though she were a poor relation under obligation, and Felicia, well, Felicia was someone she was fast growing fond of, as she might her own daughter. A sound out in the hallway made her question lightly, "Would that be your sister, dear?"

He eyed her absently and said as he moved toward the open doors. "Probably . . ." And then as an afterthought, "Amelia, won't you join us on this expedition?"

She laughed lightly. "Oh, no. I would be quite worn out long before Daphne, I do assure you. Never mind me. I have a luncheon engagement with an old friend, but don't forget, we are promised to the Waincoates tonight."

"How can I forget? Felicia has talked about nothing else all week. I hope she won't be greatly disappointed, for what she can think this particular rout will be is more than I can fathom."

"It is her *first* London rout. She is bound to be dazzled, however insipid it may be for us." Amelia smiled.

Felicia stuck her head in and called, "Daffy's coach is outside."

He smiled. She always drew a smile from him. Why that was, he could not say. Damn, but she looked fetching with that white straw bonnet framing her pretty face. She would no doubt steal hearts tonight. . . .

Much later, somewhere in the wee hours after midnight, Felicia tossed in her large bed. Sleep was impossible. Her duke, her darling, was keeping her fitfully awake. He had quite made her morning. Materials had been draped around her, styles thrown at her, and he had quietly selected his favorites. Daphne had complimented him, saying he seemed to know exactly what suited "their Felicia," for she, too, had adopted her brother's ward. The day had progressed and they had made their way to a marvelous little tea house, where they had had a perfect luncheon before the duke had asked to be dropped off at his club.

After that, there was the Waincoates' rout. The duke had declared it a modest affair. Daphne had said it was just the sort of evening to quietly introduce their Felicia before her ball. There was a select group of people present, Beau Brummell the most interesting of these. The Beau was a particular friend of the duke's, and perhaps that was what brought him to Flip's side, but there was no denying that it was her company that kept him there. She liked the Beau and was both shocked and delighted with his sense of humor. It was noted amongst all those that mattered that the duke's ward was a "diamond of the first water" and that she had quite captivated the Beau's interest. As the Beau was not easily captivated, this was considered even more intriguing than the first observation.

Felicia was not aware that she had caused such a stir. Vaguely, she had realized that people seemed to be looking her way. Laughingly, she had accepted Amelia's raving compliments, listened to Daphne declare that she would be the hit of the season. Longingly, she had gazed at her duke, but he would only smile fondly, pinch her cheek, and tell her she was his good girl. His good girl? That was not what she wanted to be to him.

She had met some young men this evening, and they had openly admired, flattered, flirted, and taken some of her attention. She had looked toward the duke, but he had not seemed to mind. Indeed, later he had laughed with Daphne and said the puppies had drooled over *their* Felicia, and wasn't that a sight to make them proud! Instead of elevating her, this statement had caused her present anxiety. Forgotten seemed to be the fact that he had kissed her, what

116

seemed now so long ago. He behaved as though she were twelve years old! And she wasn't. She would soon be one and twenty, and then she would no longer be his ward! What then, Felicia?

She thought of Scott. He had written that his father had very nearly forgiven him, and because of the duke's masterly letter to the squire, he would soon be allowed to visit. She couldn't wait. There was so much she and Scott could do in London, give some rein, that is. . . .

And on that note she finally fell asleep. It was not so for the duke, who was pacing in the library belowstairs. Felicia was driving him mad with her worshiping glances and her luscious ripe lips pouted in his direction. He was flesh and blood, after all, and not created for the role of guardian . . . at least not for a provocative female, ripe enough, old enough to be his woman! Damn. He couldn't, wouldn't think of her in such terms, but he did. He dreamed of her when he was in his bed, and his body throbbed with sure yearnings. Other women were available to him, but somehow they left him wanting. This was impossible! On that declaration he threw down a swallow of brandy and marched out of the room and went outdoors, taking up his cloak on the way. What he needed was some air! The fact that it was nearly three in the morning did not intrude on his thoughts. He was in misery. That was all he knew, and he needed some relief.

Curled up like a kitten before the fire, Felicia perused the morning paper. Her aqua-blue gown of velvet was not made for such disregard, and Amelia scolded her as she left the library in search of her spectacles. Felicia giggled and continued to sprawl. She was lazy, the fire was warm and inviting, and clothes, she declared to Amelia in the way of an answer, should be made with comfort in mind.

It seemed not a moment had passed when the Somerset butler announced in a voice that very nearly always made Felicia jump, "Miss Rebecca Wilson."

Felicia scrambled to her feet in her habitual childlike style and rushed the newcomer with glee. "Becky!"

Rebecca laughed to find herself so heartily embraced and allowed herself to be drawn into the room and planted on the yellow sofa.

"Becky," said Felicia again. "I am so happy. I did not expect you here until next week."

"No, no." Becky hastened to clarify the situation. "I am not here . . . I mean, I have not come to stay with you at Somerset House. . . ."

"What?" Felicia pulled a face. "I don't understand. I thought we had it all arranged."

Rebecca laughed. "*You* had it all arranged."

"Yes, and you did not object to my arrangements!" Flip pouted.

"That was before . . ." answered Becky with a twinkle.

"Before what?"

Rebecca was pulling off her gloves, her right first and with some haste. Her left glove she pulled off slowly with dramatic movement, so that all of Felicia's attention was centered on that hand. It produced a shriek of excitement.

"Becky! You are engaged!"

"Yes, I am, and Papa thought we should open our

London town house for the occasion and enjoy a season's routing about.'' She was smiling brightly.

Felicia was now frowning. ''Yes, but I thought that you . . . that Scott . . . ?''

''Ninny! I am engaged to Scott.''

Felicia's brow cleared and then puckered. ''Why, you dreadful brats! Neither one of you wrote me about this.''

''No, we decided you should get the news in person.'' Becky smiled and started removing her hat. ''Now, tell me, what goes on here?'' Her voice had dropped into conspiratorial notes.

Flip sighed heavily and sat down beside her friend. ''Oh, Becky . . . nothing!'' It was a wail.

''Nothing? You have been in London nearly a month and you say, nothing? What do you mean? Hasn't Lady Daphne been taking you about?''

''Oh, that? Why, yes, of course.''

''And haven't you met any interesting . . . people?'' She eyed her friend meaningfully.

Felicia giggled. ''You mean men.'' Another sigh. ''Yes, of course, but . . .''

''But what?''

''You know what,'' returned Felicia in an exasperated voice.

''Ah, your duke. Well, you can't have him, so you might as well forget him.'' Becky watched her thoughtfully as she said this.

''Becky!'' These were traitorous words! ''I love him.''

Becky hugged her. ''Oh, my poor girl. He is a man of honor and will not think of you in such terms. You are his *ward*.''

Felicia pulled away and a naughty look took over her face. "Not forever."

"It is his duty to see to it that you are presented and perhaps betrothed to a gentleman suitable enough to have you," Rebecca pursued.

"Hmmm, and *that* should help my cause," returned Flip with a laugh.

"And what is that supposed to mean?" Rebecca's hazel eyes opened wide.

"Becky, I have not spent my entire life with Scott and his friends without learning something of the male mind."

"I repeat . . ." started Becky.

Felicia laughed and hugged her friend. "You will see."

# Chapter Sixteen

All on that magic list depends;
Fame, fortune, fashion, lovers, friends:
'Tis that which gratifies or vexes
All ranks, all ages, and both sexes.
If once to Almack's you belong,
Like monarchs, you can do no wrong;
But banished thence on Wednesday night,
By Jove, you can do nothing right.

—HENRY LUTTRELL

Lady Daphne attempted to explain the importance of the vouchers she had obtained to Almack's as she went through Felicia's wardrobe, for she meant to pick out a gown for her charge for this evening. Flip looked toward Becky and pulled a face, but Becky did not respond,

"This is absurd," said Felicia. "All this fuss . . ."

"Ungrateful brat." Becky laughed. "Lady Daphne has obtained vouchers to Almack's. Don't you understand what that means?"

"Yes. We shall have to attend some stuffy dance and not waltz until the Jersey or the princess allows us to. It is not my notion of a fun evening,'' returned Felicia.

"You will not speak like that tonight,'' stuck in Lady Daphne in her threatening voice. She quite adored Felicia, but at times the child tried her patience.

Felicia moved to put her arms around her guardian's sister with great affection. "No, no, dearest Daffy. I may be rough-and-tumble, but I am not stupid, and I have a wonderful teacher. I shall not do anything to mortify you . . . no matter what temptation there may be.''

Lady Daphne eyed her and said, "Good girl. I am persuaded Glen should like you to make a good showing as well, you know.''

"You make me feel like a horse at auction,'' laughed Felicia. "But for you and his Grace, I shall not behave like one.''

"Ah, now *that* is a concession.'' Rebecca smiled.

Lady Daphne proceeded to scan the gowns at her disposal, mumbling about this one and that and then stopping as her eyes lit upon a deep pink velvet. "Ah . . . this should set your dark beauty off just so.''

"Dark beauty?'' laughed Felicia. "Oooh, I do feel exotic.''

"Felicia, don't you realize what kind of a stir you have already made amongst the beau monde?'' asked Lady Daphne.

"Nonsense,'' retorted Felicia dubiously.

"My dear, you are hailed the 'new beauty.' Why, Sir John Wingate told me that you were toasted at White's just after that Venetian breakfast we attended a few days ago . . . when you wore that pretty white-and-black muslin with the matching silk hat. . . .''

"Toasted?" ejaculated Felicia coloring up. "That is ridiculous."

"Indeed. Glen was there, for I asked him and he said he put a stop to it."

"The duke put a stop to it?" Felicia asked with some animation, wondering, hoping he had been jealous. Thus far, he had not displayed any real jealousy when she noticed him looking at some young man paying her court.

"Indeed, he said it was not fitting that his ward's name should be bandied about, even in glorious terms." Lady Daphne smiled and sighed. "It seems an age since . . ."

"Since what?" inquired Felicia for she could see Lady Daphne did not mean to go on.

"Nothing. I was just remembering my youth."

"Your youth?" laughed Rebecca. "And what have you now?"

"Middle age," groaned Lady Daphne.

"Absurd creature," cried Flip. "You are beautiful and you are young, so now what has it been an age since?"

"Since my name was toasted at White's and Freddy landed Cranfield a facer," said Lady Daphne with a giggle.

They bantered over this for some moments, as the girls wanted details and were not satisfied until Daphne had given these over. Felicia smiled and sat back against her ladies' chair and sighed. "How romantic!"

"Hmmm. Freddy has always been a romantic." She turned to Rebecca and eyed her. "What do you wear tonight, dear?"

"Aqua. Aqua-blue . . ." Becky was smiling, for

she could already see what her Ladyship was thinking.

"Brilliant!" declared her Ladyship. "Pink and aqua blue. Dusky beauty and tawny beauty. Why, it will be perfect. What a picture you two will present. You will break hearts, and my dears, we will make an entrance tonight. The doors close promptly at eleven o'clock. There is no one allowed in even one minute after eleven. Why, even Wellington himself was turned away when he arrived five minutes past the hour!" She smiled. "However, we will arrive five minutes before they close the doors."

"Why do we take a chance . . . ?" started Rebecca.

"Because this dreadful creature wants us on the block! Everyone will be within already, and as latecomers—almost latecomers—we will have an audience," Felicia said with a laugh. "I must say, Daphne, that is very tricky."

"Indeed, and why resort to such tricks?" put in Rebecca.

"Never you mind," returned her Ladyship. "You are already engaged, so you needn't worry about such things. However, the marriage mart is not lacking misses. It doesn't hurt to have an edge. Even when you have beauty, it can always be displayed to better advantage."

Almack's was full to overflowing. The orchestra played sweetly from its balcony. Corinthians were sporting a toe on the dance floor. Gossipmongers sipped their negus and whispered about the latest *on-dit*, and Felicia found it all vastly entertaining.

"Becky. Just look at that woman. Why, she is quite the most beautiful creature I have ever seen."

The duke glanced in that direction and smiled to himself, for Felicia had managed to notice his former lover. He said nothing, but his sister advised the girls that the beauty was a tart at heart and a lady by breeding.

Felicia giggled. "Who is she and why such a description, Daff?"

"She is Lady Amkirk. She married a man thirty years her senior and makes no secret of her numerous affairs."

"Ah," said Becky knowingly, "her sin is that she makes no secret of them?" She eyed Lady Daphne naughtily.

"Touché!" Felicia laughed.

They were then interrupted by two zealous young men who applied for their hands for the next cotillion. The duke in thoughtful silence watched Felicia glide away before he leaned toward his sister and said approvingly, "Felicia is looking . . . stunning this evening."

Indeed, Felicia's dusky hair had been collected into curls around her piquantly lovely countenance. One long waving strand had been allowed to escape and fell provocatively toward her breasts, which were amply displayed by the scoop of her dark pink velvet gown. The girls had made their entrance, and heads had turned just as Lady Daphne had predicted.

"Hmmm," said Lady Daphne. "She certainly will not lack suitors."

The duke frowned. "Indeed . . . it is too early to tell."

"Is it? Why, Glen, then you have not seen the way Reinhart looks at her."

"Preposterous girl!" The duke chortled. "Reinhart is a confirmed bachelor, and besides he only met her a few nights ago."

"Yes, I know, and for the last two days he has sent her flowers," she returned smugly.

"Flowers? Reinhart?" He was surprised, and he glanced toward this individual thoughtfully. John Reinhart was a wealthy gentleman who was, in fact, while not one of the duke's intimates, certainly a convivial friend. The man was something of a Corinthian, well dressed, the pink of the ton, though not titled, and as the duke looked at him now, he also conceded that Reinhart was the sort women thought handsome. Reinhart after his little Felicia? Absurd. She was not old enough. . . .

As it happened, John Reinhart was at Almack's for one reason, Felicia. Then, she had walked in and totally captivated him, so much so that he was shocked into immobility for a moment. That was time enough for someone else to claim Felicia's hand for the cotillion. Never mind, he had regained his composure, and with some style he accosted Lady Jersey and in charming accents requested permission to waltz with Felicia.

Lady Jersey smiled ruefully at him. "What is this, John?"

"She is the ward of a good friend," he answered wisely. "I should like to see to it she enjoys herself."

"Ah, for Somerset?" She smiled dubiously but allowed it just the same.

He laughed and kissed her gloved fingers. "Only if you will it, my sweet."

"Yes, John, I do, for Daphne is one of my dearest friends, and I too find this new girl . . . amusing." She drawled the last and released a tinkle of laughter.

So it was that when the waltz was struck up, John Reinhart moved across the room and sauvely took up Felicia's hand. "This dance is promised to me." He started to lead her out.

Felicia dimpled adorably and stopped him. "Oh, no, sir. This is a waltz. It is promised to no one . . . not even you." She had learned the art of dalliance quite nicely and her eyes twinkled.

"You mistake, my lovely. This dance and you have been promised to me by the Jersey." Softly he spoke.

Quickly and with some surprise, Felicia looked toward Lady Jersey, who nodded at her. Felicia blushed, but though John Reinhart was a handsome buck, she was not intimidated by him. She laughed and allowed him to pull her along, confiding in a lowered tone, "I am so glad my first waltz at Almacks' goes to you."

He smiled caressingly and returned, "Are you? Why?"

"Well, yes. I think you know enough to cover up any mistakes I may make."

He threw back his head and laughed at her candor. "You couldn't make any, Felicia. You are perfect."

"Oh, no, I am not. When you get to know me better you will see."

The duke watched the two on the dance floor and something inside of him churned. What it was he could not say. However, he could not hold back voicing something to his sister, who stood beside him watching their progress as well.

"The devil dallies with her!"

"Oh, most certainly he does, but in earnest, Glen," responded Daphne thoughtfully.

"Never say you honestly think so! Reinhart is taken with her, yes, what man would not be? But to suggest that he would throw away his freedom on a chit ten years his junior . . . ?

"Do you think that is how Reinhart see it?" Daphne was watching her brother as thoughts tumbled with questions in her mind.

"Damnation! I won't have her hurt," said the duke with some heat.

She eyed him, thinking his temper was certainly ruffled, and decided to ease into another topic. "No, and I don't think she will be." With an artful sigh she changed the subject. "I wish Freddy were here, but he can't abide Almack's. He does mean to accompany us to the theater tomorrow night." She then diverted him once more. "Oh, look, there is Ester motioning to you. Glen, go and dance with her."

"Past flames are better left in the past," he answered curtly.

"Don't be rude. Until two months ago she was not so very . . . er, past."

Reluctantly, he did her bidding, but he could not help glancing toward Felicia, who was now standing beside Reinhart and deep in conversation. Forgotten, apparently, was her guardian, her friends, all others. Damn it! This would not do.

# Chapter Seventeen

Felicia had heard quite a great deal about the Drury Theatre and the performances staged therein. Tonight, *The School for Scandal* was scheduled, and Felicia glittered with excitement as she took in all the sights. Below their box was the pit, full to the brim with London's middle class. Overlooking the pit in a semicircle, with the stage at its fore, were the boxes, and they held London's fashionables. Felicia's gray eyes took in everything, and then with unconscious glee she grabbed hold of the duke's white gloved hand and excitedly inquired, "Sir . . . sir . . . look there . . . is that the prince regent?"

He did not have to look. He smiled fondly at her and flicked her nose. "Indeed, my love. Would you like me to present you?" Inwardly, he could not help but notice that the feel of her fingers held within his own sent a thrill through him he could not explain or easily describe.

She recoiled in horror and withdrew her hand. "Faith, no!"

He chuckled and took up her fingers once more, this time putting them to his lips. It occurred to him that life had changed for him in drastic measure since the day he had met this little piece of fluff. "He won't bite you, sweetheart." And then with a second thought. "At least not while *I* am present."

Their moment was sharply interrupted by the sound of a deep male voice, and the duke found himself frowning as John Reinhart entered their box and bent over Felicia's dainty hand. "Beauty . . . you have no right looking as you do," he said in soft tones.

"Oh?" She raised a dark brow. "No right, how is this?"

"You serve as a distraction. How can I . . . how can any man engage himself to direct his attention to the play with you here?"

She laughed, and the duke made a sound something like a disgusted groan. Reinhart nodded pleasantly enough in his direction and said jovially, "Somerset . . . this is selfish of you indeed, hogging your ward all to yourself."

"It is a pleasant duty, sir, to guard my ward." There was a warning in the sound.

Reinhart's brow went up. "Indeed? She will be safe with me." He turned to Felicia and bent his arm, "Allow me to escort you to the vestibule, where I saw your lovely friend and Lady Daphne. I think you might find it entertaining and there is time before the curtain goes up."

Felicia had no wish to leave the duke, and she would not be taken where she would not go. She smiled warmly to soften her answer but shook her head. "No, I don't think so. I am enjoying myself immensely right here."

The duke almost gloated openly, but Reinhart would not be put aside. He put his hand to his heart and said in mock accents of dismay, "My lady, you wound me to the quick. Have I been sent on my way?"

She laughed and said, "No, no, you absurd creature. Do sit and join us, if you will."

"I will indeed," he said, taking up a seat on her left, leaving the duke still on her right. He claimed her attention then by taking her gloved hand. "There, look . . . see that woman in the box directly across from us?"

Felicia's eyes scanned the box and rested on a tall and somewhat dowdy-looking female in a gown that was far too extravagant for her plump figure. "Y-es . . . ?"

"That is our regent's wife," he offered confidingly.

Felicia's eyes opened wide. "But . . . they are not in the same box?"

"No, they share very little these days." He laughed.

"But they are married," returned Felicia in some surprise.

"It doesn't stop them from heartily disliking each other." He shook his head. "One day she will be our queen . . . God help us."

"That is not nice," said Felicia on a frown.

"My dear, she is not even allowed the care of her daughter," returned Reinhart on a harsh-sounding note.

Felicia looked toward the duke. "Why?"

He touched her cheek, for this piece of news seemed to distress her kind heart. "The regent allows them to dine together once or twice a week, but for

131

. . . reasons of his own he doesn't allow Caroline to raise Charlotte.''

"That is very sad," said Felicia. She looked across at the woman who would one day be queen and felt a stab of pity for her. The duke saw this and took up her hand to bring it to his lips.

Reinhart's brow went up. Well, well, here was the duke playing guardian but with what intentions? They were interrupted then by Lord Waverly, Daphne's husband, who stood aside with a merry laugh to allow his wife, Rebecca, and Amelia to enter their box. "Take them, Somerset!" said Freddy Waverly heartily. "I have had enough for one evening." Then, spying John Reinhart, he said, "Ah, you here, Reinhart? Well, time you left." He did not like Reinhart and was a man of plain speaking.

John Reinhart took this in good form, got to his feet, bowed to the ladies, and with a promise given to Felicia to call on her in the morning, made his exit. Felicia laughed and looked at Freddy Waverly, whom she already greatly liked. He was a large jovial man with few words, good humor, and a great deal of fair honesty. "Freddy, don't you like Mr. Reinhart?"

"Who said I didn't like him?" returned Freddy, taking up a seat between Amelia and his wife.

Daphne leaned forward and touched Felicia's shoulder. "He does not, never has."

"But why? I find him . . . very pleasant," said Felicia in some surprise.

"That is quite another story," returned Daffy.

"Let us hear it," put in the duke, much interested.

"Not now," answered Freddy. "It is my story and I don't mean the ladies to know about it."

132

"Nonsense, Freddy. It is time you told *me*, at least," said Daphne.

"No, it ain't." And with that he set his lips.

The curtain started to rise, which saved him some verbal battering from his company. However, the duke—for one—resolved to have an answer on this head. If Reinhart meant to court Felicia, he would have to know all about him. As of now, he could not object to Reinhart's suit. The man was plump enough in the pocket, had good standing in the ton, and . . . and hell, he would see Reinhart dead before he would allow Felicia to be his!

It had been a perfect evening. The play had been entertaining. The company had been wonderful, and the duke . . . had been fondly attentive. Felicia frowned over this last thought. Yes, he had been attentive—but as her guardian, nothing more. She hadn't been able to break through his sense of propriety and touch the man as she had back at Andover Inn. The butler let them into the house and Amelia turned to say brightly that she rather thought she was exhausted. "But thank you, Glen, that was a lovely evening." She turned to Felicia, who was just slipping off her silk cloak. "Do you come up, dear?"

Felicia knew this was more a request than a question, but she smiled and would say only, "I shall go up presently."

Amelia frowned ever so slightly. It was late, and the servants were for the most part in their own chambers. To leave Felicia alone with a man was not fitting, but this man was also her guardian. She hesitated over the problem. "Very well, but we have a big day ahead of us tomorrow, so don't be long, and do pop into my room and bid me good night when you come up.'' There. She had handled the situation to her own satisfaction and was able to turn and leave them in good conscience.

Felicia eyed the duke as he removed his hat, cloak, and gloves. He had said nothing during this exchange, and she wondered if he was going upstairs as well. She smiled at him and said lightly, ''I am starving.''

He laughed and turned to the butler. ''What do you think? Can we put together a tray for my monster?''

''No, no, Jeffries. You go on to bed. I mean to attack the kitchen,'' interrupted Felicia hastily.

The butler looked toward the duke and received a wink. ''Indeed, Jeffries. Do as our lady bids. I shall see to it that she doesn't harm Cook's kitchen.''

Felicia giggled and took the duke's hand to pull him along, chattering all the while about nonsense. The kitchen was reached and she took a moment to light a few wall sconces and have a look about. ''Hmmm. Buns! Shall I warm up some buns and make hot chocolate?''

''For yourself, madcap.'' He was moving toward the pantry closet and producing a bottle of brandy. ''Find me a glass, love.''

She produced one, and while he poured himself a glass of brandy she put on the kettle, deciding that she would make tea since she could not find the chocolate. All the while she talked in her musical voice, advising him how she and Scott often raided their kitchens at home.

He watched her, and when she stopped talking a moment in order to get an answer to an idle question she put to him, she could not help but notice the strange light in his green eyes.

"What?" she inquired, her voice almost trembling. "What is it?"

He put down his brandy glass and moved toward her. "I was just thinking . . ." He found he couldn't go on, didn't want to. All he wanted to do was take her in his arms.

Guardian be damned! He took up her shoulders, and at that incredible moment the kitchen door burst open.

"Flip! What are you doing, tearing the duke's kitchen apart?" This was followed by a hearty laugh.

Felicia turned wide-eyed and went forward. "Scott! You miserable beast, springing in on us like this, at this hour! Why weren't you here sooner? You could have come with us to the play."

He gave her a bear hug and sighed. "Lord, but you do run on, and how I have missed you." With which he planted a kiss upon her forehead, set her aside, and moved forward to extend his hand to the duke. "Hallo, your Grace. Your man said you were in here, so I left my things in the hall and . . ."

"In the hall? Whatever for? You can't sleep in the hall, dolt," said Felicia with a giggle.

He refrained from sticking out his tongue at her. He was, after all, he told himself, an adult about to be married. Instead, he said in superior tones, "Well, didn't want to have them taken up without the duke's office. That would have been presumptuous of me."

"But it is not presumptuous of you to arrive at midnight?" she teased.

He blushed and started to stammer, and the duke took pity. He patted Scott on the back and said,

"Don't pay the vixen any mind. You were invited to Somerset House, and no time was specified. However, I am certain there is a reason for all this, so why don't you take one of the buns Felicia has heated up and tell us your story."

Scott grinned and admitted that he was dying of hunger. He downed the bun in no time and reached for another. Felicia exclaimed that he was a pig and made him share it with her while she heated up another. As it turned out, he had excellent reasons for his lateness, as the post chaise he was traveling in had wheel problems and then horse problems and he couldn't get a room in any of the inns along the Post Road, as they were all booked, so he just took his chances that Felicia might still be awake.

Felicia sipped at her tea and interrupted this with a question directed at the duke. "We can give him the yellow room next door to mine?"

"No," said the duke firmly. "I rather think Scott will be more comfortable in the corner room of my wing."

"Why?" Felicia was wide-eyed. "There is nothing very special about that room."

"Isn't there? I rather think there is," said the duke, a gleam in his green eyes.

"What?" she pursued.

"Quiet," returned the duke.

"What makes it more quiet than the room next to mine?" she continued.

"That it is not next to yours." He laughed.

Scott roared and said, "Settled. The corner room it is and that is that."

She sniffed. "Oh, it is the proprieties again. Well,

that is ridiculous. Scott is engaged to marry Becky and besides . . ."

"Never mind," put in the duke hastily, for he was aware that she was about to say something outrageous. "It is time I got you both upstairs and settled before Amelia calls down a lecture on my head."

Upstairs, Felicia lingered as she watched the duke take Scott down the long corridor to the corner room. She pouted, moved across the hall, and knocked on Amelia's door to say good night. Amelia called to her, and she popped her head into the room to say, "Scott has arrived and the duke has taken him to his room. This will be so much fun!"

"Has he, dear? Well, isn't that nice." She wondered why the lad had arrived at such a late hour, but then young people were forever doing strange things. "I am looking forward to meeting him." She sighed from her bed.

"Shall I bring him to you now?" teased Felicia, bright-eyed, for Amelia was looking hysterical with her nightcap pulled low over her forehead and her gray curls sticking out in all directions.

"Dreadful child," cried Amelia, half-worried that Felicia just might do such a thing. "Tomorrow will be sufficient. Now, go to bed!"

Thus admonished, Felicia giggled and closed Amelia's door. She saw the duke had also just closed Scott's door down the long corridor. He seemed miles away. There was a longing look in her gray eyes, but though she silently called him to her, he stayed away. He gave her a soft good night and vanished to the regions of his bedchamber.

She sighed and knew it would be a long time before she would fall asleep. It was his duty to see her presented to the world, suitably matched and married to one of the ton. Well, how would she make him realize that the only man of the ton that suited her was himself?

# Chapter Eighteen

John Reinhart was looking *de rigueur* when he was taken to the morning room and announced. He found there a collection of people surrounding the object of his desires. Heads turned as his name was announced, and Felicia, who had been sprawled out on the carpet reading an excerpt from the morning paper, scrambled to her dainty feet and went forward, hands extended,

"John. Good morning to you." She smiled brightly and found her hands taken into his large ones and then brought to his lips.

She was looking radiant in a velvet gown of soft green. Her gray eyes were flecked with colors. Her black hair gleamed in layered curls, and her lips were warm and inviting to look at.

"Ravishing," he whispered.

She laughed. "Hoyden is what they call me around here, not ravishing."

"Then they are blind," he returned, still in quiet tones.

"Come on, girl, mind your manners!" demanded

Scott as he got up from his place on the sofa beside Rebecca.

"Yes, yes, or course, brat," she retorted in fine tones and then smiled again at Reinhart. She introduced him to Scott, explaining that they were friends since the cradle and that he was engaged to Rebecca. This caused the duke to frown over his morning coffee. Why did she feel it necessary to remove Scott as competition in Reinhart's eyes? Was she attracted to the man?

Felicia went on to say that John knew Amelia, Becky, and her duke and should now sit with them and be comfortable.

He declined gently. "I rather thought you might join me for a morning ride in the park. My curricle and four are outside, and I don't like to keep them standing too long."

"Your matched four?" she inquired on an excited note. "I have heard about your grays. Yes, I should like that very much." She turned to Amelia. "It is all right, isn't it?"

Amelia looked at John Reinhart, whom she rather liked, and inquired, "Your tiger, no doubt, is with you?"

"Indeed, ma'am. He is now with my horses and will accompany us during the drive."

"Then, yes. You may go, child." Amelia looked toward the duke and was surprised to encounter there a look of strong disapproval.

However, he offered no verbal objection, and Felicia skipped out of the room, exclaiming that she had to fetch her spencer and bonnet. John Reinhart then found himself engaged in a subtle battle with the duke,

"Tell me, John, you don't often take out your grays this early in the morning for a drive in the park."

"No," agreed John, "I don't."

"I take it this is a special occasion, then?"

"Indeed, I count it so."

"That, too, is not like you," returned the duke, gritting his teeth, for he dearly wanted to plant the man a facer. Odd, that—he had always rather enjoyed John Reinhart's company when chance had brought them together in the past.

"No, it is not like me, and I might add, Felicia is not like any other woman I have ever known."

"John, she is not quite a woman . . . not up to snuff. I trust you will remember that."

"As long as you do," answered Reinhart, who was now convinced the duke had more than a guardian's interest there.

"What the devil is that supposed to mean?" The duke could almost taste blood.

"Hallo . . . ready!" called Felicia, who had donned a velvet waist coat of matching soft green velvet and a top hat of the same shade, whose translucent scarf fell to the shoulders.

The duke watched her take Reinhart's bent arm, and all joy in the morning went out of the room with her.

Amelia had been watching him closely and could not refrain from asking, "What is it, Glen, don't you like Mr. Reinhart? I am certain he is thought very highly of by most of the beau monde."

"Yes, so he is, and no, I don't like Reinhart. At least, he is not for my Felicia."

"What is this? Is that top sawyer after Flip?" asked Scott in astounded accents. That a sophisticated Cor-

141

inthian should waste his time on his Felicia seemed impossible, for he thought much as a brother thinks.

Rebecca put in gently, "I think Mr. Reinhart has the look of a man . . . much smitten. He is a perfectly acceptable match for Felicia, and she likes him well enough."

All eyes turned on her, and the duke had the sudden urge to choke the life from her. She saw the duke's anguish and took pity on him. "At any rate, you may as well know that Felicia will marry where she chooses. Personally, I don't think she will choose Mr. Reinhart."

"Marry where she chooses, is it?" demanded the duke, incensed, though he would be hard put to explain why. "She will do no such thing while she is my ward!"

"Won't be your ward much longer," Scott noted. "Fact is, she can't wait . . ." He caught himself and blushed hotly.

"Can't wait for what?" the duke asked roughly. "For my guardianship to end?" He was hurt, for he didn't understand the implication. "I thought . . . I believed that Felicia was happy . . . here."

"She is," said Rebecca at once. This had gone too far. She could see the duke was on a different level. This was not what she wanted. "Scott doesn't know what he is prattling about." She turned a glare on her beloved.

"Yes, well. I will tell you this. She will not marry without my permission . . . ward or no!" said the duke, who stalked out of the room and then out of the house.

Rebecca, Amelia, and Scott exchanged glances, but it was only Scott who did not understand and asked,

142

"What the deuce is going on? Why is the duke in such a dither?"

The duke returned from his club, rigidly placed his top hat, cloak, and walking stick in his butler's hands, and inquired, "Miss Felicia . . . and Amelia are in the library?" It was a question, but as they usually were in the library at this hour, he had already started in that direction.

"Er . . ." Jeffries sensed trouble. "No, Miss Amelia went out with Miss Rebecca and Mr. Hanover shortly after Miss Felicia went out this morning with Mr. Reinhart." He avoided his employer's eyes.

"Did they? Then, Miss Felicia is upstairs?" He was frowning.

"No . . . Miss is still . . . out." Jeffries hestitated over every word.

"The devil she is!" thundered the duke. "Do you mean to tell me Mr. Reinhart has not seen her home yet?"

"Yes, your grace." Jeffries' words were scarcely audible.

"But it is nearly one o'clock!"

"Yes, your Grace."

"They went out at ten o'clock."

"I believe so, your Grace."

"I'll have his blood!" roared his Grace.

The front door opened and there stood Miss Felicia. She had her back turned to them as she had moved to wave good-bye once more to Mr. Reinhart, who was seated in his curricle. She laughed and turned to discover the duke looking a storm and Jeffries slinking into the background.

"Hallo! I have just had the most enchanting morning," she beamed and began taking off her bonnet.

"Have you, my girl? Have you, indeed? Well, it is no longer morning and we will have to discuss . . . your morning. In the library, if you please," demanded the duke, who then made her a mock bow and indicated that she must precede him.

His anger was most evident. That she had done nothing to warrant it bolstered her, so she smiled sweetly at him and attempted to soothe him. "Of course, your Grace." She swept past him in regal style, giggled, and began removing her spencer. He flung open the library door, allowing her to enter first, and then closed it at his back.

She looked up at him all wide-eyed wonder, for now she knew there could only be one reason for such a temper, and it was not because she had stayed out longer than she should.

"What is it, dearest sir?"

"Don't you know?"

"How should I?"

"You have been out with Reinhart for three hours and want to know what you have done wrong?"

"I did not do anything wrong. He took me first to Hyde Park, and then just outside the city to show me his team's paces. We met dreadful traffic on the return trip and I am ravenous. Shall we go in for lunch? Where is Scott?"

"I am the one asking the questions!" he snapped.

"No. You are the only one getting answers," she returned on laugh. "Where is Scott?"

"He and Rebecca are out with Amelia," he returned stiffly. He took a moment to level a fulminat-

144

ing eye upon her and added, "Properly chaperoned, I might add."

Felicia gazed at him naughtily. "Ah, so if Amelia is with them, then you and I . . . are not properly chaperoned?" She had moved closer with each word and was pleased to see something she could almost name in his deep green eyes.

"Don't change the subject," he answered, but his tone was less sharp than it had been only a moment before.

"I haven't. . . ." She came closer still.

"You don't need a chaperone when you are with me," he put in to stop her, stop himself. "*I* am your guardian."

"Ah . . . so you are." She moved her hands slowly up his chest and her lips parted as her eyes met his.

He grabbed both her hands and stopped her—forcefully, almost angrily. He was a gentleman of honor. He couldn't, wouldn't give in to his animal cravings. That was all it was that he was feeling. Wasn't it? Damn! He wouldn't let these sensations get the better of him. She was his ward, under his protection, and principles dictated that he keep his distance. "Felicia . . . I repeat . . . I am your guardian—your chaperone, if you will. Nothing more."

Had he slapped her, he couldn't have wounded her more. She dropped her gaze and felt her heart quiver within her body. His words echoed in her mind so that she couldn't hear anything else. He was saying something more, but she couldn't hear him, didn't understand the words. They were meaningless words after those last. *Nothing more.*

She controlled her trembling lips and managed to say, "I . . . I am . . . tired. . . . I think I will go to my room." So saying, she turned and made the supreme effort to walk, and it was an effort, for she dearly wanted to run. She didn't, though. She took the stairs in ladylike style, walked down the corridor to her door, opened it, and went to her bed. However, at this point she lost control, and as she dove into her pillows, her young heart burst. He was her guardian . . . nothing more. Words enough to explode a young girl's dreams.

# Chapter Nineteen

Dinner that evening proved to be a sorry affair. Scott and Rebecca managed with Amelia to keep up a steady flow of conversation, but the usual merriment that accompanied these meals was lacking. Felicia did not mope, but gone was the twinkle from her gray eyes. She smiled at all the appropriate moments. She spoke when addressed and in hearty enough tones, but her friends could not help but know that something was wrong.

The duke was preoccupied and left the house immediately after dinner. Felicia asked Amelia idly where his Grace was off to, but she did not know, and Scott answered without thinking, "He is a man about town. Don't you think he is entitled to go off with his intimates, or does he always have to dance attendance upon you?"

Felicia bit her lip. She wouldn't cry. Rebecca kicked her beloved in the shin and told him that he was a stupid fellow.

"Why? What the devil did I say?" He was actually puzzled.

"Never mind," said Rebecca, putting an arm

around Felicia and saying quietly, "No doubt the duke went off to his club. He didn't look as though he wanted a night's revelry but a place . . . to think."

Felicia went into total depression. "Someplace away from me."

"Yes, but for reasons you cannot understand at the moment," answered Rebecca quietly.

"I don't know what all the fuss is about," put in Amelia, frowning. "I must say, his Grace has been on his best behavior because of our Felicia. He was wont to go every night to his dreadful hells and dives. Why, his sister told me that he hasn't been near one all month, and what is more, I don't think he is going to any of those places tonight, either." She shook her head. "Now, go and play at something. I want my stitching."

They smiled at her, and Felicia made the effort at conversation, cards, and mild entertainment until well past nine o'clock. She then announced her intention of going to bed. Scott saw Rebecca home, and Amelia also went up to her room. Felicia washed and sat by her fire for another hour before sighing and climbing into her bed. She hadn't heard him come home. Where was he? Who was he with?

She tossed, turned, and finally fell asleep, but she was sharply awakened by the sound of someone stumbling in the corridor. She got up and ran to open her door in time to find the duke, one shoe on and the other held in his hand as he leaned into the wall. He smiled at her. "Hallo, madcap. You up?"

"You are foxed!" accused the lady.

"So I am," grinned the man.

"Oh!" Felicia lost her temper and slammed back into her room. That he had been out apparently drink-

148

ing and having a jolly good time was beyond everything annoying. Well, so much for her blue-devils. If
that was what he wanted, so be it! She would just go
on with her life and marry . . . with which thought
she felt an urge to cry once more. She did not, though.
Instead, she turned and forced herself to sleep.

Morning breakfast proved to be a strained affair,
for neither Amelia nor Rebecca was there to help the
situation. Scott looked from the duke to Felicia as
they exchanged clipped remarks and attempted to stay
clear. Inadvertently, he added fuel to the already-too-
hot sparks.

"So, you never did tell me . . . how was your ride
with that Reinhart fellow? Heard tell his matched
grays are quite something to look at."

Felicia's eyes gleamed. "Indeed, Scott. They are
a beautiful gray and move together superbly, but then
John is a whip with great skill. I enjoyed watching
him handle the driving reins immensely."

"Humph!" said the duke. "John, is it? And let me
tell you, I know Reinhart's style with those horses
and it is all flash. If he met real trouble, he wouldn't
be able to handle it. The man can drive . . . but not
to an inch!"

"Oh, really?" retorted Felicia, color in her cheeks.
"And you can?"

"Do you doubt it?" The duke was near to shouting.

Scott's eyes were open wide. "Of course she
doesn't doubt it, do you, Flip?" He looked at her
hopefully.

"I don't know." Flip shrugged her shoulder.
"Some men are all talk."

Scott nearly choked and attempted to repair this

149

with stammering sentences. The attempt was lost, for the duke and Felicia were glaring hard at one another.

"Is that what you think, that I am all talk?" his Grace demanded.

"I think that you probably are in a temper because of your . . . convivial evening."

"And even so, I can outdrive . . . outride your wonderful Reinhart!"

"You have a very high opinion of your skills," she returned blandly. "Do others share it?"

"What matters is that you will share it when I am done!" He got up and moved to his bellrope. A moment later his butler appeared, and he said in forceful terms, "Send to the stables. I want my high-perch phaeton and my bays . . . the four of them!"

"Yes, your Grace." Jeffries made a quick exit.

"Go and get your cloak," he ordered Felicia without smiling.

"Gladly!" she answered sharply and moved with some haughtiness.

"Zounds," breathed Scott. "What the deuce is wrong with you two?"

"Never mind!" snapped the duke, who turned on his heel and followed Felicia out of the room.

It was some twenty minutes later that the duke was coldly but gallantly helping Felicia into his high-perch phaeton. He turned to his young groom and lightly dismissed him. Felicia eyed the duke sardonically.

"Don't we need your groom . . . as a chaperone?" And then quickly, before he could say it, "No, no, how stupid of me. *You* are my chaperone."

He said nothing to this as he climbed up beside her. His lips were set in hard lines and he avoided glancing her way. That she was looking stunning in her black velvet driving ensemble with the gold frogging was something he did not want to dwell upon. Instead, he gave his full attention to his team and the bend of the road.

Felicia adjusted her black velvet top hat and could not refrain from honestly exclaiming, "Faith, but I must say . . . your bays are magnificent. John's snowy grays are flash, but your bays are certainly every inch blood!"

He returned no answer to this, though quietly, silently, he felt slightly mollified. The streets they had passed were quiet ones, and though he handled his reins skillfully, nothing yet had called for precision driving. However, he had to add, "Yes, and Reinhart's vehicle is not designed for the speed mine can produce when tested."

She shrugged a delicate shoulder. "No? He seemed to take it fast enough."

"Did he, indeed?" returned the duke, whipping up his horses. At this juncture a knot of traffic was met, and he forgot his grievances as he gave his attention to tooling his team and vehicle through the intersection.

Felicia lost her anger as she watched him. He was wonderful. His skill at the reins was something she admired as much as his handsome looks. Everything about him drew on her soul. She waited until he had executed his turn and allowed him in animated tones, "Oh, Glen, you are most certainly a notable whip!"

Suddenly he laughed. "And not moments ago, it is very nearly what you said of Reinhart."

"Yes, but you *do* outshine him," she admitted. "As you said, he does not drive to an inch, but . . . you do." She blushed and looked away.

"And of course you consider yourself judge enough to know?"

He was teasing and was surprised to see her return with some heat, "Indeed, sir, I do!" Her cheeks felt hot, but she did not look away this time. "My father was such a fine whip . . . there was none like him . . . except perhaps yourself, and I managed to learn a thing or two at his side."

"Did you, by God?" He looked at her in mild surprise. "Well, then, here!" He was handing the reins into her gloved hands.

"No . . . no . . ." she objected, horrified.

"Show me what you can do," he demanded softly.

"No, no . . . not in this traffic." She gave him back the reins.

He relented and said, "Very well. We will move out of this traffic."

He proceeded to the Post Road, asking her questions all the while about her father, her early years with him, with her stepmother, and found that her memories were all fond ones. She had worshiped her father and had been close, very close, to her stepmother. She talked freely, affectionately about them, about some of their times together, and in that manner the next thirty minutes passed swiftly.

The sun was just beginning to peep from a clouded sky, and Felicia exclaimed that she couldn't believe such a beautiful landscape was just a short distance from the hub of the city.

"Don't you like London?" he inquired, brow up.

"Well enough, but I rather think I miss the country," she said wistfully.

"Then after your ball we shall have to go to Somerset. It is in the New Forest, and I think you will enjoy that."

"Yes, if you don't have me engaged to someone by then," she retorted and then giggled outrageously.

He pulled a face at her and handed her the driving reins. "Here, vixen, show me your stuff!"

# Chapter Twenty

It was the night of the ball, and Felicia looked at herself in the long looking glass. Her gown of white and silver suited her provocative curves. The pearls at her ears, threaded into her dark curls and around her neck, suited her station, and her loveliness was enough to steal the breath away, but she pouted over her reflection, wishing she were older, more womanly, more sophisticated. So much had happened since that morning the duke had allowed her to drive his team. They had drawn closer in so many ways, but she had not succeeded in breaking through his barrier. When he would forget and affectionately touch her or take her hand, he withdrew suddenly as though he had touched a flame.

What was she to do? Reinhart had been courting her diligently, and though she knew the duke disapproved, she was not able to break his veneer of parental concern. She had even teased him on one occasion, declaring that he was jealous. He refuted this with heat, and she had retreated again into the blue-devils.

Now, she would have to descend the stairs and

enter the beau monde officially. She could hear the music sweetly playing and the buzz of company already festive. She would soon be one and twenty and he would no longer be her guardian. What then? He seemed to want her safely married, yet whenever the subject came up, he changed it. What could she do?

"Felicia?" It was Lady Daphne with Amelia at her back. "Come, love."

Well, it was time. She released a long sigh and said quietly, "Yes. I am coming. Is Becky downstairs?"

"Everyone is downstairs, you stunning creature"—Daffy laughed—"so don't look so glum. Have you any idea what a picture you present?"

"Oh, Daffy. I hate this. I wish I were home." Felicia had a sudden urge to run.

Lady Daphne took her arm. "Buck up, my dear, this is not like you."

"Yes, it is," insisted Felicia.

"You will be surrounded by people who love you and by people who want to get to know you and by others who will be envious . . . and you will know how to handle them . . . and yourself," said Amelia confidently. "I know."

And on that note, they went before her to await her beside the duke at the bottom of the stairs. Slowly, Felicia followed. It is a frightening thing to make one's entrance for the first time. Felicia felt herself tremble as she realized that so many eyes were watching her progress down the main staircase. She found the duke's eyes and suddenly felt bolstered. As she completed the distance to his extended hand, she felt caressed by his gaze, warmed by his smile, and all others faded.

155

The duke had seen her at the top of the stairs and his heart had very nearly stopped beating. She had been encased in an aura of light, and he had felt his blood race through his veins, had felt better than he had ever felt in his life. She was more than beauty, she was life.

Her gloved fingers were clasped in his own, and he led her into the ballroom. There was a sudden short hush before the buzz of conversation proceeded. A waltz was struck, and the duke was the first to lead Felicia onto the floor. As he moved with her in perfect grace, she smiled at him and could not help exclaiming, "I cannot breathe."

His green eyes twinkled. "It seems we are overcome with the same problem. I lost my ability to perform that function the moment I saw you at the head of the stairs." He shook his head sadly. "I will lose you tonight. . . ." His chin indicated a collection of young men ready to claim her hand as soon as the dance was over.

She laughed. "Oh, Glen. You never claimed me. How, then, can you lose me?"

"That is the second time this week that you have used my given name. I wish that you would do so always." He had changed the subject again.

She frowned. "Does one call one's chaperone by his first name? I think that would not be quite the thing."

"I have checked the rules. It is acceptable," he answered softly.

She looked at him long then, and said in a small voice, "You are quite breaking my heart."

He laughed this off. "Why? Because I want you to address me by my given name?"

"You know why, and still you mean to give me away," she answered without smiling.

"Felicia, my own dear girl, what you feel for me . . . will pass. Putting you in the limelight is my duty as your . . . guardian. I want you to meet all the eligible men there are in England and have your pick of them."

"I have already met a great many men and you do not like any of them. John Reinhart you say is not right for me. Young Stewart you said is a fool and Oscar hasn't enough . . . what was it you said, yes, not enough experience to make a good husband. You object to everyone who has come calling. Who, then, my own beloved duke, shall I have?"

"We shall see" was all the answer he could give her, for the waltz had ended and Reinhart was already waiting to claim her hand. He watched her go off with Reinhart and gritted his teeth. This was what he wanted—well, not Reinhart precisely, but someone like him, better than him. Damn! No one was good enough for her.

Ah, Felicia. When she looked at him he almost believed there was something real in her eyes, but he didn't believe in love. He knew too well that love in a young girl's eyes quickly passes, moves on to someone new. If he allowed himself to feel . . . he could be hurt.

It was better this way. Her infatuation would pass as soon as her interest was locked elsewhere. She would soon be one and twenty and no longer his ward. What then? Well, he had wanted her to have her pick of men, and as he looked around he could see that she certainly had that, and for some reason this did not cheer him in the slightest.

The evening was drawing to a close and Rebecca was frowning. Scott saw the expression on his true love's face and inquired, "Oh-oh. What are you up to?"

"I am going to dance with the duke."

"Are you, precious? Why?"

"Never mind," she answered and pinched his cheek. She moved in her gold silk with some determination and came upon the duke. His back was to her as he conversed with an old friend, and she had to tap his arm to get his attention.

He turned and smiled at her. "Hallo, sweetheart," he greeted jovially.

"Dance with me . . . I think there is enough of the waltz left for us."

"With the greatest of pleasure, but the gossipmongers will have cause to chew the fat, my dear. This will be our third waltz this evening."

"Good, poor dears need something to talk about," she returned with a smile and allowed him to lead her onto the floor and into the step.

She had to find a way of talking to him without stepping beyond the line, and without making matters worse. She had to present him with the facts, not the solution. The solution was a thing he must come to on his own. Slowly, she said, "I have come to know Felicia . . . very well."

He eyed her. "Y-es. . . ."

"Enough to know that she knows her own mind. In fact, once she has made up her mind, it is a difficult thing to move her."

"Your point?" He was eyeing her intently.

"My point is that she will choose her own husband and that choice will be the right one for her."

"What are you trying to tell me? That she wants Reinhart and I must stop putting a rub in their way?" He was frowning.

Rebecca groaned. He was thick at times! "No. If she wanted Reinhart you would know it beyond a shadow of a doubt and therefore would not really be able to put a rub in their way. Why don't you take a good look at Felicia and listen to what she has been telling you. What she wants and what you want . . . are so very . . . close."

"And what does she want?"

"Don't you know, your Grace?"

He frowned then and looked at her hard. "I am not certain that I do."

"Really?" Rebecca's tawny brow was up dubiously.

"Indeed, Rebecca, for I am not sure *she* knows what she wants."

"Then, your Grace, you have not been listening to me, which leads me to believe you have not been listening to her."

The waltz was over, and Scott had come to claim her hand for a cotillion. The duke watched her for a moment, a furrowed line forming across his forehead. Suddenly he felt a soft touch cross his brow and a musical giggle.

"Such a dreadful frown! What has you annoyed? Surely not my own dear Becky?" Felicia had seen them waltzing together and knew the count as well as any of the gossipmongers in the room. While she was not quite jealous of this, she was certainly curious.

He smiled at her and caught her ungloved fingers and put them to his lips with a short laugh. "There is nothing you two girls could do to make me frown."

It was Flip's turn to laugh, and she nearly roared in an unladylike fashion but restrained herself and dimpled. "I think, my beloved guardian, you have not thought that statement out." And then mischievously, "May *I* have a third waltz?"

"No," he said and tweaked her nose.

"But Becky had one. I think we should set a new trend," she retorted naughtily.

She was always hard to resist, impossible to deny, and he was never immune to the charm she could so readily display to advantage. "Very well, monkey, but they are playing a cotillion."

"That . . . can be easily changed," she declared in high glee. "It is, after all, *my* ball!" With this she hurried off in gliding easiness, and a moment later a waltz had been struck up, much to the astonishment of most of the people on the dance floor.

Much merriment ensued as the dancers moved into the steps of the waltz and Felicia pulled her chosen partner along. She giggled all the while, only stopping when he had her in his arms and her gray eyes found his deep green gems shining at her. "You have such . . . beautiful eyes," she told him softly.

"No, my love, if you want to understand beautiful, you must look in the mirror at your own," he returned.

She sighed happily. She had this moment. She had the feel of him near, the aroma of him, the sound of him. Tomorrow . . . was something she would worry about tomorrow.

Rebecca waltzed by on Scott's arm and smiled at

them. Look at them, she thought. How was this dratted situation going to end? Was he blind? Was he so cold-hearted that he didn't feel what he must be feeling? Wasn't he in love with Felicia, or was that look just a . . . a fatherly show of affection? Bah! Fatherly, indeed!

## Chapter Twenty-One

Lord Waverly eyed his lady as he helped her out of their town coach and said in an undervoice, "She is going to put up a fuss. Mark me now . . . and I don't like fusses!" He turned to his coachman and told him, "We shall probably be twenty minutes." Then to his wife, "Well, let's get it over with."

Lady Daphne Waverly sighed. "The trouble is, Freddy, you are right. You are always right."

He patted her hand. "Dear love, don't fret it. We'll muddle through."

"Yes, but are we going to just stand by and . . ." It was at this juncture that her mouth dropped open and nothing more filtered through, for they were passed by a young man who was well known to them.

The young man came dashing out of the house they were entering, muttering something about a duel. He stopped and mumbled something in the way of greeting and the fact that his life was now over before he dashed past them and down the street.

"That was young William," said Freddy in some surprise. "Seems a bit distracted."

"Oh, no, Freddy. He can't have stopped William

of Hartsford from courting Felicia!" wailed Lady Daphne, much exasperated. He is an earl, he is wealthy, and his family . . . why . . ."

"Loose screws, the lot of them," announced Freddy. "But can't deny . . . they are ton."

"Freddy, it is dreadful. The Jersey had a talk with me yesterday afternoon. She said that the duke has sent all Felicia's beaux packing. Said that he won't let anyone court Felicia, and it is looking strange."

"Well, she turns one and twenty tomorrow. He won't have any say about who courts her then."

"No, I suppose," returned Daphne on a frown.

The double doors of Somerset House were open wide for them and they were taken through the central hall, down the corridor, and announced at the open library door. Within, a charming picture met their gaze.

The duke was seated by the fire on the yellow sofa, his paper folded in his hands. Felicia was sprawled out at his feet on the hearth rug, a cup of coffee at her elbow and a fashion plate open at her fingertips. She was reading the duke a severe lecture about something. She looked up and found Daphne and immediately enlisted her aid.

"Daff! Good, you are here. Do you know what this brother of yours just did? I am so embarrassed."

"Never mind," returned the Duke on a frown.

"He sent poor William out of here, saying that he wasn't fit to stand up for a waltz with me let alone court me!" said Flip, ignoring his command.

Daphne blanched. "Glen, you did not do that! Glen, tell me you did not do that."

"I did do that and it was true," said the Duke of

Somerset irritably. "How dare that puppy come after Felicia!"

"Glen . . ." started Daffy.

"Hush, my love," said her husband. "What is done, is done. You will take young William's mother out for tea tomorrow and repair the damage." He eyed his brother-in-law. "Can't go about insulting bloodline like that, Glen. Causes your sister some social discomfort."

The duke eyed Freddy and grunted. It was all he meant to say on the subject. He knew he had behaved irrationally with young William, with all the men who had come asking to court Felicia. He hadn't meant to behave in that fashion, but he felt none of them suited her. He didn't want her forming an attachment for some young man who wouldn't make her a good husband. "I'll ring for coffee," said the duke and got up to move to the bellrope.

"Felicia, do you know why we are here?" It was Lady Daphne pulling on Flip's hand and bringing her up to her feet. "Come, sit with me on the sofa and we will talk."

"What?" Felicia looked rather suspiciously. "What is wrong?"

"Wrong? Why nothing." She patted a place beside her and waited for Freddy to sit opposite them. She could see that her brother had retreated to a window. "Tomorrow you will be one and twenty."

"Yes, isn't it wonderful?" Felicia smiled.

"Indeed, but my brother's guardianship will be at an end," continued Daphne gently.

"Yes," said Felicia happily.

Daphne was surprised. She thought that Felicia rather adored her brother. She looked at her husband

and then proceeded. "So, my dear, we . . . Freddy and I both . . . would like you to come and stay with us for the remainder of the season."

Felicia's face fell and she stumbled over her next sentence. "Leave . . . leave Glen . . . here . . . I . . . but . . ."

"It wouldn't be seemly for you to continue here, now," said Daphne gently.

"That is absurd," retorted Felicia with feeling.

"So it is," agreed Freddy. "But Daffy and I enjoy your bubbling company so much. Couldn't you manage to put up with us?"

Felicia's mind was already at work. Would she see the duke anymore? Daphne's town house was no more than a ten-minute walk away, but there would be no mornings together, no late evenings in the library near him. But she would no longer be his ward. No longer his ward! Now *that* was something.

"Thank you. I should love to come and stay with you for the rest of this season, if Freddy promises to tell me why he does not like John Reinhart."

Freddy grimaced. "I don't make deals with impudent children."

"Yes, but Freddy . . ." started his wife.

"Never say it is settled, then?" returned Freddy, interrupting her. "There you are. There is never outguessing what a woman will do. Thought she would put up a fuss. You did, too, Daffy. Glen thought we were going to have to drag her out of here."

"Yes," put in the duke. "I thought she might not want to leave me." His voice was tinged with hurt.

"Ah," said Felicia mischievously. "Freedom is a funny thing, the yearning for it can make one want to leave almost anything."

"And anyone, it would appear." Definitely, the duke was hurt.

"One must move on," said Felicia quietly. "Everything must change." There was an adult gravity to her voice, belied only by the twinkle in her gray eyes.

"Well, there you are!" exclaimed Scott from the open library doorway. "Rebecca and I have been waiting for nearly thirty minutes in the dining room!"

"Why were you waiting there?" Felicia was surprised.

"Came in at the same time . . . William of Hartsford arrived. The duke sent us to the dining room to wait for you," explained Rebecca.

"Well?" asked Scott anxiously, for there wasn't time left to waste.

"Well, what?" returned Felicia on a laugh.

"The balloon, girl, the balloon. Have you forgotten?"

"Oh, faith!" Felicia jumped to her feet. "I'll just fetch my bonnet and cloak." She turned to the duke. "Are you coming?"

He shook his head. "I think not."

She stomped her foot. "But you said you might."

"I find that I cannot," he lied.

"I see." She put up her chin, much annoyed with him. Some minutes later they had made their farewells for the morning, and the three young people were off to witness a balloon ascension.

"I suppose," said Daphne, "that is that. It leaves only her things to be sent to our home."

"Yes," said the duke, strangely quietly. "It leaves only her things."

# Chapter Twenty-Two

Waverly House was built, furnished, and designed with modern fashion in mind. Every room was decorated with style, elegance, and good taste. However, as Felicia meandered from room to room she found she couldn't make herself comfortable. Then she discovered Freddy's study.

She peeped in and was immediately drawn by the warmth and simplicity of the room. Here, now, was her kind of surroundings. It was dominated by its fireplace, a stone structure of considerable size. Bookshelves lined the walls, but the books that were stored there were all in great disorder. Felicia felt comfortable with that. The furniture was covered and cushioned in brown velvet, the hangings were made of the same. The room was designed with a man's sense of comfort, and the tomboy in Felicia liked that as well. So it was that she took her morning coffee and planted herself by the fire, advising Freddy to go on with whatever he was doing at his desk. She wouldn't bother him, she assured him.

He eyed her in some fascination, for this was his private sanctuary. No one had ever dared invade this room before, but she looked rather adorable in her pink velvet gown, and there was something of the kitten in her as she sat in front of the fire, so he let her remain, grunting mildly and returning to his paperwork.

She waited only a moment before advising him in a conspiratorial voice, "I am hiding." She pushed away her coffee and waited for his reaction to this.

He knew he shouldn't ask, but he couldn't stop himself. "Why? From whom?"

"From Daffy."

"Ah, yes." Now this was something he could understand. He adored his wife, but at times one did have to hide from her.

"It is my birthday today. I am one and twenty, and she has been fussing over me since eight o'clock this morning."

"Good God!" Again he sympathized with her.

"Hmmm. She means to take me out this morning, but I don't want to leave yet."

"Don't you?" Again he told himself not to ask, but couldn't help himself. "Why not?"

"I think that Gle—the duke will be here soon . . . and I want to see him."

"Fond of him?" asked Freddy, unable to hide his interest in her answer. Here, now, was a mystery easily solved. The girl was in love with the duke.

"Yes."

"I believe he is here now," said Freddy quietly, getting to his feet. He could see he would get no peace this morning. Might as well open his doors and let them all in. He could hear them looking for Felicia in the hall outside. He moved to his closed door that no one before Felicia had dared to violate and stuck his head out. "Looking for Felicia, my dear?" To the duke he nodded. "Hallo, Glen."

"Why, yes, have you seen here?" asked Daphne in surprise.

Freddy stepped out of the room and closed the door at his back. "She is in there."

"With you? Alone?" His wife's brow was up. She was, after all, a woman.

"Indeed," agreed her brother. "What the devil do you mean closing yourself up with Felicia alone?"

"Don't be absurd," returned Freddy in perfect calmness. "She was hiding, came in there to hide from Daff."

"From me? Why?"

"Doesn't want to go out. Wanted to wait for the duke," returned her husband.

"Yes, but I wasn't expecting Glen," said Daffy in puzzlement.

"No, but he *is* here." To Glen he said in a strange voice, "It is time, ol' man. Go in there and wish your ex-ward a happy." To his wife he said, "Come along."

" 'Come along.' What do you mean, 'Come along'?"

The duke watched Freddy pull her away and drew a long breath as though to bolster himself before he entered Freddy's study. There she sat, her pink velvet skirt spread around her provocative figure, looking like a dream, with her black shining curls in profusion to her shoulders and her cherry lips beckoning.

She saw him. It was what she had been aching for, needing with her entire being. He was everything. He was her world, and she ran to him and clasped both his hands. "So, here you are at last!"

"Happy birthday, brat," he answered on a laugh. By God, how he had missed her. Had it been only one day, one night that she had been away? All day yesterday, all through the night he had longed to hear her laughter, wondered what it would be like not to hear her laughter again. He couldn't bear the thought.

She giggled happily and kissed the knuckles of his hand, saying softly, "I was so put out with you yesterday. I wish you had spent the day with us at the balloon ascension. It was ever so nice."

"I am sorry for it. I wish I had been there with you. We will make up for it today." He suddenly held her to him. "The house was empty without you."

"Quieter, you mean." She was dimpling up at him, looking deep into his green eyes, calling a response from him.

"Felicia . . . I can't . . . don't wish to think about what my life will be without you there."

"You needn't. Shall I move back and we can live in sin and scandal?" She was teasing but she was daring him to go on.

"I have never felt this way before." He made his declaration. "I suppose I am doing this badly, saying it all wrong?"

"Yes, you are. Do it right, my love. Say it better," she commanded in dulcet tones.

"I love you, Felicia, and I want you to be my wife." He dropped a light kiss upon her waiting lips. "How was that?"

"Good . . . good . . . but I will show . . . you . . . one better," she murmured, and proceeded to do just that!